Dark Visitor

By Madsen Pirie

Arctic Fox Books
London

Arctic Fox Books

First published in Great Britain in 2007
by Arctic Fox Books, 23 Great Smith Street, London

ISBN Number: 978-0-9555844-1-1

Typeset in 11pt Baskerville

Cover design by Tony Fleetwood

Printed by Biddles Ltd. 24 Rollesby Road, Hardwick
Industrial Estate, King's Lynn, Norfolk PE30 4LS
Registered in England and Wales No. 00158041

FOR ROBYN GREENROD

CONTENTS

Acknowledgements

When I was a boy I chanced upon a copy of Isaac Asimov's Foundation in my local library. I was captivated by the audacity of its vision, and by the sweeping imagination of its author, and became an enthusiast of science fiction. I discovered there was a huge range of books, including several that were specifically written with children in mind. One after another I devoured as many of them as I could find, and spent hours of my adolescence in the company not only of Isaac Asimov, but of Robert Heinlein, Arthur C Clarke, and the great names of the genre including the classic writers, H G Wells and Jules Verne.

My first acknowledgement, therefore, is of my debt to the masters of science fiction, to those I have mentioned by name and to the countless others who enriched my youth. Although science fiction is usually combined with fantasy into the category of Fantasy and Sci-Fi, the two are quite distinct. Science fiction itself seems to form only a small part of that category today, especially in children's books. Stories which involve the technology of other worlds seem to feature rather less than those which involve warlocks, sorcerers and magic stones or fabled swords. The authors I read wrote about children whose experiences fell within the realms that science does, or might one day, allow, rather than about magic which does not. I follow that tradition.

My second debt is to the long-suffering friends who have read the early, unpolished drafts and made helpful suggestions. John Hutchinson, Jonathan Woolham and Paul Woods have patiently read my work and offered advice and encouragement. It takes a very special talent to see in the first draft of a book the work it might ultimately become. Fortunately I had Rick Dickerson, who took time off from his own writing, to help me with that.

I must especially thank Catriona Wilson of the Circus Literary Agency, who took the time and trouble to coach a novice writer in some of the crafts of the trade. Rachel Wade helped with brilliant editing suggestions. The longer this list grows, the more I appreciate how supportive and patient so many people have been.

My final debt, I suppose, is to those who helped with the production of this book, so I acknowledge the help of David Cuthbertson, who designed the appearance of its pages, Steve Bettison and Tom Clougherty.

This book was immense fun to write. It came almost fully formed into my mind from somewhere in the inky blackness of deep space. A cadet sits out her solitary watch on the space station, when suddenly a minor alarm sounds off, and things start to happen... I hope my readers enjoy it, and I welcome their comments, criticisms and suggestions.

1. The Dark Ship

The single tone of a bell echoed along the station's corridors, waking Laurel from her daydreams. She shook her head awake, and turned her attention to the status board.

Laurel knew there was something wrong immediately. Ships don't dock unannounced. They radio their presence in advance. You see them hundreds of thousands of miles away as they enter the system from deep space. Their transponders alert the station's computers so they can be identified and given a carefully controlled approach trajectory. Even if they are trying to evade detection, you see them on radar. The station detects their approaching energy signal. The big lumbering cargo freighters might take days to approach, and even the sleek little courier ships gave several hours' warning. Ships just don't dock unannounced.

Laurel was also certain no ships were due that night. Her first task on watch was always to check the status board and schedule the approaches, an easy task on a night as quiet as this. Sitting in a remote arm of the galaxy, the Auriga system was not a busy place. One freighter was taking a leisurely trajectory around the star, scheduled to dock in almost two days' time, but otherwise there was nothing. She finished the dregs of her coffee and rubbed her eyes. Clearly she should arrange for a technician to check the rogue bell.

1

Glancing down at the status board again, she froze in disbelief. A single light was lit up on the panel, announcing a ship was docked. Laurel knew this was simply not possible. There was no ship in the system close enough to dock. She stared at the board, the single yellow light staring back like a malevolent eye. Obviously there was no ship; there couldn't be. But she would have to check.

She called the bridge, and a fresh-faced young man came up on the screen, smiling. It was Blake.

"Hey, Laurel. Trouble on watch? Things getting too exciting for you?"

He was joking, of course. Watch was just about the dullest job on the station.

"Two malfunctions on one watch. I'm overwhelmed," she told him with a wry smile. "Bell and light both say there's a ship docked. Obviously there isn't, but I'm going down to South dock to check."

Blake frowned, and glanced briefly down at something out of view.

"I confirm there have been no incoming ships. Call me when you get there and I'll note it for engineering."

Laurel signed off, pulled on her jacket and left the watch room under control of the station computer. South dock wasn't actually in the South. The station floated in a distant orbit far beyond the planet, so there was no South. On the station, it meant the dock on the down side of the station's gravity field, underneath the station. It was a short walk down the corridor and through the recreational park, one of the few places on the station where the oily, metallic reek of the corridors retreated, giving way to the fresh scent of grass and flowers. In no hurry, she meandered around the trees, touching the bark with her fingers as she passed. Above her the branches stretched up to the large glass dome, beyond which hung the dark infinity of space.

1. THE DARK SHIP

In the two years since she had joined the station, at the age of twelve, she had grown used to seeing the park's daylight disappear above her into the blackness of space. One thing she would never grow used to, though, was the sight of her home planet, Akron, hanging in the sky above, a brown and white globe half-li§t by the rays of the distant star. Until she came to the station she had spent her entire life on Akron. It was quite something to gaze up at her home planet whenever she took a walk. It contained everything and everyone she had ever known in her first twelve years.

Staring up, she could just make out the mountain range that was home to her parents' settlement, at the edge of the shadow creeping across the surface of Akron. It would be evening for them now. She imagined them brewing tea by the fireside after their meal, relaxing in their comfortable armchairs and telling each other about their day. She felt a pang of homesickness, thinking how comfortable those evenings had been, nursing a glass of warm milk by the fireside while her mother plaited her hair, her father discussing the day in his soothing voice. She missed their reassuring presence.

Laurel shook her head. As homesick as she sometimes felt, she knew it was an illusion. She could never be happy going back to that life. Akron was a small and sparsely populated planet, where nothing new or exciting ever happened. One day was much the same as the other, and in truth Laurel had become rather bored of those evenings by the fireside, her parents rehashing the same stories, covering old ground. The station might be even smaller, she thought, but at least she was connected to the rest of the universe. Ships came and went from all over the galaxy, from exotic places that she had only read about. She had met people who had seen things she couldn't imagine and one day, once she had graduated from the station, she could go and see them for herself.

Laurel remembered her parents' response to her announcement that she had passed the tests, and the station was willing to train her for space work.

3

"Leave the planet? Leave the planet!" her mother had exclaimed in disbelief. "I can't even imagine you leaving home!" Her mother and father had spent weeks trying to talk her out of it, but ultimately realized it was futile. Their daughter had a thirst for adventure that they could not quench.

Of course, there was a second motive for leaving the planet that Laurel could not tell them. Part of the station's allure was that her parents weren't on it. On Akron she was an appendage to her parents, the Mackays' daughter. On the station she was herself, Cadet Laurel Mackay, apprentice in the space academy and trusted member of the community. Ships and people came and went, and new things were always happening. Even things as trivial as a signal malfunction.

She made her way through the corridors to the far side of the park and headed down to the South dock. The fragrant scents of the park faded, replaced by the vague smell of engineering which lingered throughout the corridors.

The docking area was deserted. With no ships were due, there was no reason for anyone to be in the area, except for herself, the watch officer checking on a phantom signal. Laurel picked up a halogen torch and made her way systematically along the hangar bays. Everything seemed to be in order. She reached bay six and smiled instinctively as she saw her reflection in the door's window. Young she might be, but she still looked the part of the officer on watch. The olive tunic with its high collared jacket added years to what might otherwise have been an impish face. The tunic's colour was a good match for her eyes, she thought, offset by the floppy fair hair. She straightened up to add authority to her reflection, then grinned inwardly at the absurdity of her gesture. She shrugged; there was work to be done. She cupped a hand around her eyes to peer through the window, and relaxed when she saw nothing, until it occurred to her that something was wrong. She should have seen the stars through the open outer doors.

That was the problem, then. The outer door had somehow closed itself, setting off the rogue docking signals. It hadn't

1. THE DARK SHIP

happened before but, Laurel reasoned, was nothing peculiar. She checked the bay pressure and opened the door to get a closer look. As her eyes accustomed to the gloom inside, she took a sharp breath and stared in disbelief. A ship.

It was black. Its torpedo shape was utterly featureless. No fins, no windows, no markings of any kind. It was big, too. Stretching the full length of the bay, up to the closed outer doors. Laurel found herself shivering as she gazed at it. The ship was profoundly black. As though it were radiating darkness. Sinister. Menacing, even.

Laurel walked around the ship, trying to comprehend what she was seeing. It had entered silently and unannounced. Laurel was sure there had been no energy signature or any kind of trail, and certainly no communication. This mystery added to its darkness. It had slipped in from deep space without registering its presence until it docked.

It was not a type of ship Laurel had seen before. She looked it over carefully for any kind of marking or identification. There was none. There was no name, no serial number, nothing. There was no sign of a crew, either. Could they be watching her now? She felt her breath quickening and made an effort to control herself. This was silly. It was just a ship. All right, it was a pretty strange ship and it wasn't giving much away. But a ship was a ship. Science. Nothing inexplicable.

She shone her torch at it, hoping to pick out some surface detail. She clucked impatiently when the torch beam failed to appear. She must have picked up a dud. She played it on her own hand and saw there was a beam. But when she turned it back towards the ship there was nothing. It was no brighter, just the same smooth matt black surface.

Laurel looked down to check the power gauge on the torch and saw that it was falling even as she watched it. The ship was sucking power out of the torch battery. No wonder the ship looked so dark; it was absorbing the light that fell upon it.

Laurel had no idea what could do this, perhaps some unknown metal or polymer. Its surface showed no grain or sheen. Tentatively she reached out a hand towards it. As her fingers touched it she snapped them away as a sharp pain seared through them. That was silly. She looked at her fingers and saw with dismay that ugly weals had already appeared on the tips. The ship's surface had not been hot; this was a frost burn. The ship had sucked the heat from her fingertips. She licked her fingers to soothe the throbbing.

The lights above were flickering first paler, then brighter. With a start Laurel realised the ship was sucking power out of the hangar bay lights, draining their power cells, just as it had done from her torch. She dashed outside, shut the door and turned off the bay lights.

Shaking with the unease this strange ship had caused her, she stopped to recover her composure, forcing herself to breathe more regularly.

Her communicator activated. It was Blake. "Hey, Laurel. Having fun with the malfunction?"

She sighed. This was too big for her. "We need to wake the captain."

* * * * *

"Two days of diagnosis and testing, and we have no readings of any kind on any instrument. The ship does not respond to broadcasts made at any frequency on any channel. The body of the ship does not respond to explorative tests using radar, infra-red, x-ray, electro-magnetic probe, spectrographs or interferometers. The surface of the ship cannot be sampled for chemical testing. After two days we know precisely what we did before. Nothing. Zero." Blake's face showed bafflement and exasperation in equal measure.

"You've tried everything?" Laurel asked in disbelief.

"Laurel, it doesn't even respond to a punch." Blake held up his fist, tight red weals scarring his knuckles. He allowed himself a smirk. "I'll admit, this is becoming intriguing as well as frustrating."

Laurel could see some of the results of his efforts. His freckled face was streaked in grease and oil. Sweat had matted his ginger hair across his forehead. He took another swig of chilled juice and shook his head in resignation.

"An enigma stops being fun when there's no solution to the puzzle. The problem is that it sucks up everything we try on it, so we can't get any signals back. It's effectively a very neatly shaped black hole."

He leaned back against the bulkhead wearily and tossed back more of the juice.

After radioing for help, Laurel had watched the research team enter the dock in their white isolation suits and gloves. She had easily spotted Blake because he was the youngest member of the group, and had an unmistakable gangling look about him as he moved. She herself had been herded straight into a decontamination booth, where she'd spent most of the past forty-eight hours being showered, probed and monitored for various contaminants. Ultimately both she and the ship were given the all clear when it was conceded the ship could not be emitting anything dangerous since it was emitting nothing at all. Laurel was frustrated to have missed the early excitement following the arrival of the ship, although Blake was happy to fill her in.

He was, she supposed, her best friend on the ship. They had both been recruited into the space academy from Akron, although Blake was a few years older than her. Whilst she was recruited for her graphic and communication skills, Blake was a natural engineer and it was widely predicted he would have a long and prominent career once his training was complete. Although they had few common interests, they liked to spend time with each other and shared a fascination with the unknown.

7

"So all we know is that that it's so cold it burns," Laurel remarked, nursing her own fingers in sympathy.

"It isn't even cold," Blake said. "The ship absorbs all forms of energy: heat, radiation, light. When you touch it, it literally sucks the heat straight from your fingers. Even short-term exposure could be lethal."

"Is that it? You know, Blake, if you don't find something new soon, your fan club is going to start losing interest."

Blake laughed, "There's only so many ways we can tell them we know nothing." His work had never been so popular before and, even though he was a junior member of the team, his profile on the station had become huge. Wherever Laurel went, station personnel were talking excitedly together and watching the screens for progress reports. The research team's efforts were carried live, and crowds had gathered outside the docking bay hoping to catch a glimpse of the ship itself. This was by far the most exciting thing to happen since a malfunctioning freighter collided with the station and tore open three docking bays. In fact this was more exciting, Laurel realised, because it had the thrill of the unknown about it.

"So, strictly off the record of course, what's the best guess?" she asked. Engineering was not her subject, but it was his. His opinion counted for more than most. Blake's hazel eyes clouded over as he thought about it.

"Well, it's a ship, obviously."

Laurel smiled impishly. "Obviously," she said with mock gravity.

"No, I mean… it's something built. It's been made for a purpose. It uses different technology. Not necessarily better, but different."

Laurel's eye's widened. "You mean it isn't human?"

"Maybe. Maybe not. I think it comes from deep space. It probably uses quantum space like we do to bypass light speed, but if it's a research ship, it's a very strange one."

1. THE DARK SHIP

"That's an understatement," Laurel agreed.

Blake nodded. "There are no external instruments, no windows. It's as though the ship isn't interested in what's outside it. Whatever is inside is pretty well shielded. Nothing gets through. Its cargo must be pretty precious." It made sense.

Any further thoughts were interrupted by an on-screen announcement from the head of the station's research team, Dr Eliot Benson. He would hold a full station-wide press conference in half an hour.

"They found something," exclaimed Blake. "And during my break too. You coming?"

Laurel tossed him an incredulous look. Of course she was going.

"What do you think they've discovered?" she asked as they headed towards the briefing room.

"Knowing that ship, it could be anything," Blake mused. "Nothing would surprise me."

* * * * *

Dr Benson stood at the lectern, waiting for the auditorium to fill up. He was in a thoughtful mood, dark furrows beneath his shock of white hair. Laurel tried to read his expression, but all she could read was worry.

He began by clearing his throat, even as the last few latecomers were still slipping into the room. Laurel noted, not for the first time, that he was not a natural communicator. He failed to make eye-contact with the audience, addressing the empty space above their heads. He came over as remote and detached, which she thought was fair enough. He was a scientist, not a politician.

"Let me summarise what we know. For those who haven't been following the case," he permitted himself a nervous smile. "Precisely fifty-two hours ago, an unknown ship docked with the station. Its approach was not detected. We have since concluded that this was because it absorbs most all forms of

9

energy, and therefore is undetectable by any of our standard equipment. Nor did it respond to our standard signals."

Dr Benson pressed a button, and a schematic of the hull of the ship came up on the screen behind him. "The ship is of a type unknown to our records. We have tried to examine beyond its hull, but it has proved opaque to all our conventional probes." Benson paused and wiped a few beads of sweat from his forehead. He looked uncomfortable, Laurel thought, either because he was not used to being in the spotlight, or perhaps because there was something else. It transpired there was.

"We have been working around the clock on this, with only one discovery." A silence fell across his audience, and Laurel felt Blake stiffen beside her. "We have detected, from somewhere inside the ship, a low energy sound pulse which causes a tiny resonance." He gestured to one of his assistants, who played with his equipment until the sound reverberated throughout the auditorium. Thump. Thump. Thump.

"As you can hear, it is a rhythmic sound, regular and repetitive. I stress that what you are hearing is not the pulse itself, but our magnified rendering of its resonance. It is extremely low energy indeed." Benson looked more comfortable now. This was science he was explaining, and he warmed to it.

"If you look at its beat on the oscilloscope," he said, gesturing to a green line which appeared on the screen behind him, "you will see that each beat is identical in strength and timing, and in the decay pattern of the sound." He punched his palm in time to the beat. Thump. Thump. Thump.

Laurel felt uneasy. The rhythm was oppressive and, like the ship itself, there was something extremely menacing about the sound.

"Do we know what is causing his noise?" asked one of the station newscasters.

Dr Benson wiped his forehead, flustered. "That we do not. Indeed, the ship has proven otherwise impenetrable." He stared into space over his glasses. "We did rather well to pick up even that."

"And you have no idea what this might be?" the newscaster asked him again. The bluntness of it threw Benson.

"It could be any regular mechanism. I'd say the chances were very high indeed that it's a timer."

The room went very quiet, but Dr Benson was oblivious to the effect of his words. "Yes, a timer," he mused, almost to himself. "It's counting time."

"What is it timing?" the newscaster asked, this time very slowly and quietly.

"Oh, it could be anything," Benson shrugged.

"Could it be a bomb?" This was from one of the other reporters. Benson paused, lost in thought, and only then did it dawn on him what he was saying.

"Well, yes. Oh dear. We cannot rule out the possibility."

Pandemonium broke out in the auditorium as everyone dashed for the doors to spread the news.

2. The Sound

The sound reverberated through the station. Thump. Thump. Thump. Laurel thought it had been unwise to leave the sound on the station's speakers while the research team tried to probe its origins. It generated unease throughout the station. How could people go about their ordinary tasks with the constant beat in the background? Although Laurel did not think it likely that such a mysterious and unique ship as this would contain anything as mundane as a bomb, it was still an oppressive sound, a constant reminder that something alien had entered the station.

Laurel was in the canteen, eating lunch and watching the exploration live on the monitors. There was Blake with the rest of the team, his face screwed up in concentration, determined not to miss any excitement by taking another break at the wrong time. He kept her in touch from time to time with what was going on.

On the screen, the engineers carefully attached four vibrator packs to either side of the hull of the ship. After a number of unfortunate experiences, everyone in the bay wore thick space-quality gloves when around the ship. Laurel licked her fingers absent-mindedly. They were still pretty sore.

Blake had proudly explained what they were doing earlier that day. "It occurred to me that if sound can escape the ship, then we can use sound to probe the ship." he told her, "Indeed, sound is the only form of energy which seems to pass straight through the hull, so we're using it to put together a picture of the inside of the ship. When each pack sends out a pulse, the others detect it, and from the interruptions to the sound we build up a picture of what the inside of the ship looks like."

The thumping sound from the ship came relentlessly over the speakers even as Dr Benson called a pause to the work and came on screen to explain his progress so far. He looked a lot more at ease without a live audience, and talking on straight scientific matters.

On the screen, schematics showed the picture they were gradually building up of the inside of the ship. Although it seemed to have compartments and engines of some sort, none of it was familiar to Laurel.

"This is what we're particularly interested in," Benson said, pointing to the outline shape at the core of the strange ship. "We don't know what it is, but it seems to be where the rhythmic sound is coming from." Laurel felt misgivings again as she looked where Benson was pointing. It was a container of some kind. It occurred to her it could easily be the casing for a bomb.

Laurel spotted something else strange. She leaned forward and pressed the com-switch. "Dr Benson, will you take a question?"

Benson looked startled. He blinked. "Who is this?"

"This is Cadet Mackay. The ship came in on my watch."

"Ah, very good. What is it?"

"There's no sign of crew on the ship," Laurel remarked.

"Indeed. We suspect it came in on autopilot."

"But there's no sign of crew *quarters*." Laurel had seen over enough ships to know that there had to be places for the crew to

14

eat and sleep and to shower and exercise. Of this there was no sign.

"I suppose so," said Benson, surprised, "I hadn't spotted that. Perhaps it's some form of scientific probe."

Dr Benson pushed up his glasses, glad to have got to the bottom of that. However, Laurel saw the implications even if Benson did not, and they were not good. No crew quarters meant an automated ship, which could easily be a missile. The timer also indicated it might be a bomb. She became aware again of the throbbing noise. Thump. Thump. Thump.

She decided it would be better to keep these speculations to herself for now.

* * * * *

Work developed well over the next few days, and Laurel spent all of her breaks, and some of her quieter shifts, following the progress. Once the ship's layout and structure were worked out, the team moved on to using ultrasonics on the container within the ship itself. This was a very delicate process, since the sound pulses had to be focussed together on the exact spot. Laurel watched enthralled as a perspiring Blake helped the others to position and calibrate each vibrator pack before sending the pulses. Laurel heard the *ping* of each sound pulse, amplified for the audience.

Very gradually, a picture began to emerge.

"That's the timer," Blake called out excitedly, his eyes wide as he watched the outlines take shape. The timer moved with each *thump*, which still reverberated over the speakers.

Like everyone else on the ship, Laurel was gripped by the spectacle. The timer was right at the centre of the ship, within the container itself. There was no sign of the hard outlines of metal, or of any wires or other components.

Thump. Thump. Thump. It moved with relentless regularity and precision, but no-one knew what was it doing.

Benson's voice came over. He spoke as if he were thinking aloud. "No electricals, no joins, no hard edges."

Laurel stared at the thing vibrating on the screen. At the back of her mind was the thought that this was familiar, but she couldn't place it.

Benson continued to narrate, still thinking aloud. "Although it has the precision of a timer, it actually bears some of the characteristics of a pump."

His words triggered a memory and led Laurel to the elusive thought. She knew what it was. She leaned forward again and pressed the com-switch. The entire station was listening as she spoke to the scientist.

"Dr Benson, I know what that is."

"Yes, Cadet Mackay?" The man was startled.

"Dr Benson, it's a human heart."

* * * * *

Everyone on the ship was talking about Laurel's discovery. She noted wryly that opinion was divided. Some, like Dr Benson, were generous in their praise, whilst others made their jealousy so evident that Laurel could almost feel it radiating from them. She decided the best policy was to courteously thank those who showered her with praise, and courteously agree with all of those who didn't.

The whole mood on the station was more relaxed now they had established that the ship was not a bomb. Indeed, the presence of what was now universally referred to as 'the visitor' was exciting, and the steady beat, which had once seemed oppressive and menacing, was now the source of much anticipation.

It was the speed which had fooled them, as the heart was beating well below normal speed. Although everyone had a different explanation for this, Laurel believed Blake's explanation was the most likely. "The heart has been

16

deliberately slowed down. Whoever it is has been put in a deep sleep – suspended animation. Just enough metabolic activity to keep them alive without using much energy."

Someone inside that container was in suspended animation. That meant they had been on a long voyage through quantum space. A really long voyage.

Laurel continued to follow the team's progress with the ship. The visitor was subjected to detailed sound scans, and a picture of what they were dealing with gradually emerged. The visitor, like the heart, was clearly human in form. The computerized image built up from the various scans showed a figure covered by protective clothing, and sealed within the pod which apparently sustained its reduced life systems.

There was another thing which Laurel could not help noticing from the images. The visitor was not only human; he was decidedly male.

Dr Benson had gone up in Laurel's estimation. He might be a poor communicator, and too wrapped up in his work to see how it related to other things, but he knew how to run a science team.

"We have three targets, and I want three teams," he'd told them. "First team will find how to open the ship. Second team will discover how we can open the capsule. Third team will prepare the means to revive and sustain the occupant. Get to it and keep me apprised." It was clear, logical and to the point.

Blake, to his disappointment, had been assigned to Team Two, to help open the capsule. "I'd rather have been first into the ship," he confided to Laurel. As it turned out, Team One was even more disappointed.

Just as the ship had proved impervious to energy probes, Team One found the ship's hull impenetrable. Because of the way it sucked up any radiation, lasers and heat lances had no effect. No tools or blades were found to be sharp enough or fine enough to make any impression upon it. The team knew from the ultrasound scan how thick the skin was, but they had no way of knowing what it might be made from. The matt black surface stared back at them impassively, defying them to make headway against it.

From the computer's construction of the ship's interior, the team was able to locate a logical place for a hatch. Sure enough, when even finer sonic pulses were used, a hairline appeared on the graphic roughly where they had surmised. But no means of opening the hatch was identified.

It was just as Team One was running out of ideas, every tactic frustrated before it could begin, that the ship solved the problem by opening itself.

There was no sound, no hiss of air. One moment the surface was smooth, black and impenetrable, the next an opening appeared. It caused pandemonium as the station's emergency procedures activated automatically. The hangar doors swung closed, trapping the team inside the docking bay. A klaxon screeched and a disembodied voice alerted whoever might be listening to a breach of quarantine.

"Blake are you in there?" Laurel spoke into her communicator, and was greatly relieved to hear his voice. Then his picture appeared.

"Yes, but there's no problem. A hatch opened but there's no pressure difference, so air is neither rushing in nor out."

"What's it look like inside the ship?" she demanded. Blake looked aggrieved.

"We don't know yet. We have to check the inside environment before we can enter. We have no idea what might be waiting for us."

It took only half an hour to establish there was nothing to worry about. The probes reported no toxins, no biological hazards, no radiation. It seemed safe to enter. Dr Benson had the honour, but the entire station was glued to events on their monitors, following his every step.

The halogen torch, which had showed no effect on the outer hull, provided good light inside. The ship's interior showed no sign of absorbing radiation like the outer hull. It struck Laurel that the inside of the ship was bare and clean, unlike her own living quarters which were strewn with possessions. The ship almost antiseptic in its cleanliness. Her earlier observation about the lack of crew quarters fitted. It was clean and tidy because nobody lived here. There was none of the random clutter, the debris of human habitation.

Benson meanwhile was making steady progress into the heart of the ship. He shone his torch over the next threshold, and paused when he saw what was caught in its bluish light. Across the station everyone else paused. Picked out in the beam was the source of the pulsing sound which had mystified them for so long.

It was a silver capsule, its surface scattering crazy distorted reflections of the torch beam across the walls. Within it, they knew, was the solitary beating heart of their visitor. Laurel shuddered slightly, and suspected she was not the only one. The capsule looked like a silver coffin.

Blake was delighted that his team would be involved so soon. "Maybe it will open itself when it's ready, like the ship did?" Laurel suggested helpfully, but one glance at Blake's scowling face told her that this was not his preferred outcome. He would rather help solve the problem.

The gleaming container was carried to the isolation unit, one of the wards set aside in the event of an interstellar pandemic. Thankfully it had never been needed for that purpose, only for the occasional incoming passenger with a transient infection. Team Three had prepared it rigorously as a containment centre. Force field and bio-filters were set in place to guard against any biological material escaping from the unit. Even the visitor himself, should he take it upon himself to move without clearance, would find impenetrable restraints at every turn. It might be called an isolation ward, Laurel reflected, but it was a prison in all but name.

Blake's team probed every detail of the pod. They quickly established the structure of the life-support systems, and found the seams along which the capsule would open, but there were no external marks or mechanisms or switches.

During one of her breaks, Laurel discussed the latest findings over lunch with Blake in the park. "We have to reason it out," Blake told her. "There's no-one else to open it, so either it will open automatically, or the visitor himself opens it. But to do that he must be awake. Either way there has to be a mechanism which ends the deep-sleep, or which opens the pod. All we have to do is find it and trigger it."

Laurel thought Blake was missing the true puzzle. Why was a sole passenger travelling in deep sleep through quantum space in a ship designed to fly without a crew? What reason would he have to wake?

"Maybe there's a time limit?" she suggested. Blake looked blank. "I mean, the ship's systems can only sustain him for so long before it needs to resupply." It sounded rather lame when she put it like that.

Blake looked doubtful. "How would it know where to put in? Or where might be hospitable?" Laurel shrugged. There were too many questions and too few answers.

It was Blake who finally found the solution. The scans had found what appeared to be a control box inside the pod, in reach of the passenger. Blake reasoned that if the visitor was awake, he himself might open the pod from the inside. Blake thought that if they could activate the controls from outside then the pod might open.

"Why don't we beam a high frequency sound pulse at it," he suggested to his team leader, "and vary the frequency to see if we get a response."

2. THE SOUND

The team leader, a balding fellow who was well-liked by his colleagues, looked doubtful, but he didn't want to discourage new ideas. At this point they were desperate for solutions. He nodded, and Blake set to work.

Laurel watched the operation on screen. Blake raised his eyebrows when he was ready, and received a curt nod in reply. She couldn't tell what was happening to the sonic pulse or the control box, but she could see Blake's face light up in amazement. He looked up in delighted surprise.

"It moved," was all he said.

His team leader snapped fingers and motioned. The crew drew back quickly, Blake included. There was an audible click which Laurel and the other enthralled watchers could hear over the sound feed. The top half of the capsule smoothly separated from the bottom and slid to the side. The pod was open.

In the subsequent chaos Laurel caught only a glimpse of the pod's occupant. It was enough to make out a prone figure in a silver bio-suit and helmet. The team leader motioned his crew backwards and shouted "Team Three!"

The new team, clad in protective suits, took up their positions in the isolation area as Blake's team pulled out. The leader pointed to the camera.

"Cut feed," he said, and the screen went blank.

* * * * *

It was two days before Laurel was allowed to see the visitor. She practically blackmailed Blake into taking her to see Dr Benson and, to her surprise, Benson was more than happy to let her see the visitor. As he explained, it was she who first greeted the ship, it only made sense that she should be allowed to see the visitor too.

"However," he explained, "you're going to have to talk with Dr Lindberg too. I have no authority over him."

Laurel felt her victory snatched away. Now she had to convince Jeffrey Lindberg, in charge of bio-containment. Not good. Lindberg was nobody's fool. He was a great scientist. He was even rumoured to be in the running for a Nobel Prize. It would take more than downcast looks and fluttering eyelashes to win him over.

To Laurel's surprise it proved far easier than expected. Lindberg was an impressive figure. From those dark eyes thoughts flew like arrows. She could almost feel the man thinking. But he was surprisingly affable and was completely at ease with himself. He must have been about her father's age, with a few wisps of white showing just above his ears. His skin glowed with vitality, and he looked like someone on top of his profession.

"Ah, you're the girl who recognized the human heart. Splendid." The smile came on. "What can we do for you?"

Laurel outlined her request, and was surprised when Lindberg nodded.

"Yes, why not? Can't keep everything secret." And that was it. Once she had been dressed in an anti-contamination suit, Lindberg led her personally into the isolation unit.

She didn't know what to expect, but the reality astonished her. The visitor was still wearing his silver bio-suit, but his helmet and gloves had been removed. Laurel gasped. It was a boy.

Somehow she had expected a full-grown man. Complex quantum ships were not the kind of toys boys played with, but the sole occupant of the ship, still asleep, was a boy of about Laurel's age. Maybe fourteen, maybe fifteen. His skin was so dark. He was almost coffee coloured. What gave his age away was the smooth complexion and contours of the face. Time had worked no havoc on the fresh features. The close cropped hair was jet black, as were the eyebrows. From the closed eyelids came curly lashes, but the giveaway was the upper lip. The lips themselves were full, almost mauve in colour, and above the pronounced bow of the upper lip curled a few dark wisps of black down. This was a boy on the brink of manhood.

His breathing was deep and rhythmic. Laurel was astonished. This didn't look like suspended animation. She asked Dr Lindberg about it.

"Over the course of two days the pod has gradually moved him out of deep sleep. The breathing has picked up, as you so astutely noticed, but so have the heartbeat and temperature. We don't have to worry about how to resuscitate him; it's happening automatically." Lindberg casually picked up the boy's wrist and felt his pulse. "Right now he shows all the signs of ordinary sleep. I wonder if he's dreaming?"

"Is it safe for you to touch him like that?" asked Laurel. It might expose both of them to unknown risks.

"Oh I think so," Lindberg replied. "You can never be sure, of course, but we've scanned thoroughly for anything that might damage either of us."

Laurel felt almost mesmerized by the sight of the sleeping boy. There was something magnetic about the dark stranger. She watched the chest rising and falling with the rhythm of the deep breathing. Then it changed.

"Dr Lindberg!"

"I see it, I see it." Lindberg was alongside her looking intently at the boy. He held an optical instrument over the boy's mouth and nose. He backed off suddenly as the lips twitched. The breathing stopped. The whole body jerked briefly, then relaxed again.

Laurel was staring at the eyelids as they flickered, and suddenly snapped wide open. She found herself locked into a gaze with the most alien eyes she had ever seen. They were a fierce bright amber, and the contrast with his dark skin was stunning. The boy stared straight into her eyes.

The lips moved, and the boy, without taking his eyes off her for an instant, said, "My name is Van."

3. Bright-eyed

Back in her quarters, Laurel stared at the picture Dr Lindberg had given her. The visitor's bright amber eyes stared out at her from that dark face. It was unreal, unlike anyone she had ever known. Of course, she reflected, she lived in a remote and under-populated solar system, which had only experienced two or three waves of settlement by outsiders. The Auriga system was scarcely a melting pot of human variation.

She went over to her monitor and brought up the station's genetic database, a system she'd used occasionally at work when screening some of the more exotic pets brought onto the station by the crews of interstellar freighters. In theory the database held genetic information on all known species and variations in those species, including humans. She tapped in the visitor's photograph and ran a check for any matches. It was as she had guessed. No close matches. There were two near matches and about thirty or so fair matches. She knew from experience that fair matches were worthless, so called up information on the two near matches. She immediately saw that neither was human.

One was a speshka from one of the planets of Lyra IV. Its huge yellow eyes stared impassively from under bushy eyebrows. The beast was supposed to personify wisdom, but it didn't need to be all that wise to live on a diet of shellfish. They weren't the hardest prey to catch.

The other was more interesting. Laurel tensed when the image appeared. It was a tiger from Earth. It was, in truth, nothing like the strange boy in the isolation unit, but there was something Laurel saw in it. Although it had eyes of similar colour, Laurel realised a greater similarity was that the tiger emanated the same aura of danger. She watched a short clip of a tiger stalking its prey through the jungle. It looked awesomely deadly.

The database included a short article by Professor Peter Ringeld, a natural history specialist at one of the academies. Laurel skimmed it, and was surprised to find some lines of poetry about the animal. It had been written on Earth, where humans had first developed. The poet was called Blake, and she wondered briefly if her friend had been named after the poet, then smiled at the idea. She had met Blake's parents and could hardly imagine a less poetic couple. She read the lines.

Tiger, tiger, burning bright

In the forests of the night.

She shivered slightly at the thought, suspended in space countless millions of miles from Earth, of a tiger stalking her through a dark forest. As she flicked off the monitor and prepared for bed, she pondered the words at the end of Professor Ringeld's article, "the tiger may look beautiful, but it is well to remember that it is essentially a predator."

These lines were still echoing in her mind the next day as she sought out Dr Lindberg. Perhaps it was time to put some of her misgivings to rest. In truth there was nothing she could put her finger on, just a general background of unease.

Lindberg glanced up and smiled a welcome as she entered his office. Laurel looked round.

"Where's Van?" she asked. Lindberg put down the charts he'd been examining.

3. BRIGHT-EYED

"In the isolation unit."

"But you said there was no risk of disease or contamination."

"Sure, no risk in a purely biological sense." Lindberg seemed thoughtful. "We just think he might be safer there until we've found out more about him."

"So what do we know?" she asked.

"Why don't you ask him yourself?" suggested Lindberg. "I'm going over to see him now, and it might even help if you tagged along. My face is all he's seen recently, and he seems pretty bored of it."

Despite herself Laurel was looking forward to seeing the strange boy again. Something told her they were not even close to getting to the bottom of his story. As she and Lindberg walked through the station to the isolation ward, Lindberg warned her to be ready for surprises. This only served to sharpen her appetite and intrigue her even more. Mystery upon mystery; what was it about Van?

Quite a crowd had accumulated outside the entrance to the ward. Fascinated station crew keen for a glimpse of this latest stage in the story, Laurel supposed. Additional guards had been assigned to the isolation unit's entrance, and several new security measures had been installed. She wondered briefly which was the greater threat; that the crowd should get in, or the visitor should get out.

Lindberg led her into the isolation unit. The room was comfortable but clinical, sparsely decorated. The visitor's amber eyes immediately locked on to Laurel. Van stared straight into her, and she felt he was evaluating her, assessing any threat she might pose. Determined not to be intimidated, she stared right back. She began to suffocate in the tension of the moment, and was almost hypnotised, uncertain whether she could now look away even if she wished to. She was rewarded with a small victory when the boy backed down first by turning to Dr Lindberg when he spoke.

"Van, this is Cadet Mackay," Lindberg said.

"Laurel," she said, smiling.

The boy nodded briefly to her.

"Your ship came in on my watch," she said, proudly. "You've been quite a news event on the station."

The boy said nothing, but continued to gaze at her in his penetrating fashion.

"Does he not speak?" she asked Lindberg, discomforted by the boy's silence.

Van stood and walked around his cell, stopping with his back to the two. "Perhaps I just have nothing to say," he said.

"Our young Van is quite the charmer," Lindberg said, "Especially with the ladies."

Laurel did not feel things were going well.

"Does she know?" Van asked abruptly, but without turning round.

"No. I thought perhaps you would like to tell her," Lindberg suggested, but noting Van's silence, continued. "You see, Laurel, it seems Van has no memory."

"Specifically," Van interrupted, turning round at last, his eyes resting on Laurel. "I know that my name is Van, but I don't know anything else. So perhaps you see now why I don't have much to say?"

"You don't remember anything else?" Laurel was incredulous. This sounded both strange and unlikely. The boy shook his head.

"It's true," confirmed Dr Lindberg. "When we found he couldn't tell us anything we ran a neural scan. His memory has gone, and he didn't just lose it. It's been erased."

Laurel drew breath sharply. "Erased?"

"Yes, deliberately wiped."

3. BRIGHT-EYED

"You don't remember anything at all?" she asked Van.

"Catch on quick, don't you?" Van said sarcastically. He yawned theatrically and sat down on the hardback chair in his cell.

"It's really more complicated than that," Dr Lindberg explained. "Van clearly remembers how to walk and talk, and neither of us knows how he comes to speak our language. He remembers those basic skills he will have learned at some stage. It's the higher memories which have been erased. He has no memory of past events, of people and places."

Laurel's mind raced as she took it in. So yet again mystery was compounded with mystery, and even Van did not appear to know the solution. The boy had arrived alone, in suspended animation, from somewhere in deep space. And he had no idea where he was from, who he was or why he was here.

"How come you know your name?" Laurel asked him.

The boy laughed dryly to himself, "You may wish to keep up. I don't know how, because I don't remember *anything*." Laurel was surprised by how quickly Van turned to anger. He was utterly uncooperative with the only people who were in any position to help him.

"Can't you look at the ship's records?" she asked Lindberg. "If he can't tell you anything, then they surely will. The ship must know where it came from, how long the journey took?"

"I'm afraid it's not that simple," he said. "Our science team looked over the ship's records, but they've been erased too." He looked thoughtful.

Laurel caught a flash of distress in Van's face, but it was gone as quickly as it came, and he regained his fearless façade. "Someone has gone to a great deal of trouble to get me here, and an extraordinary amount of trouble to prevent me knowing why."

"Indeed, from our point of view the latter question is the most serious." Lindberg mused, "We really would like to know why you're here."

Van lapsed. into a sullen silence. Although Laurel thought he could show better self-control, she was developing a sympathy for the boy. He was lost and utterly alone, with no family, no friends and no memories.

Lindberg picked up his sheaf of charts. "Of course we can tell some things about you. There may be no records in your memory or in the ship's log, but there are records in your body. Life leaves its marks." Van looked up.

"Like what?" he asked.

"Like your bone growth," replied Lindberg.

Van shrugged. "Bones grow," he said dismissively.

"Not like yours they don't." Lindberg brought up an image of a femur on screen and magnified a cross section of it. "Look here," he pointed. "Your bones show negligible growth in seven years."

"Seven years!" Laurel was aghast. "He's been seven years in quantum space?" This was mind-boggling. Even the longest trips involved a few weeks of deep sleep at most. But Lindberg was not finished.

"Before then there was growth of perhaps a few weeks only, and before that another gap. And the pattern is repeated."

"What does it mean?" asked Van. He looked more forlorn and confused than angry now. Lindberg leaned back.

"We can't be certain," he reflected, "but it looks as though you have been on a number of deep space voyages. Your memory and the ship's records have been erased. Maybe it's happened several times. The thing is that I have no idea why."

Laurel's instincts had been right. Van was utterly strange. This was a mystery within a mystery.

The amber eyes looked intently at Dr Lindberg. "Anything else?" Van asked him quietly. The scientist looked him over very thoughtfully.

3. BRIGHT-EYED

"Well, there's DNA of course. I tried for a match on your DNA, but there's nothing like it. You're not from anywhere we know about, that's for sure." Lindberg fiddled with the screen controls until the familiar double helix appeared. He put it into huge magnification.

"You have human biology, obviously, but the problem is with the junk DNA." He pointed to the screen. "This is the stuff that replicates itself without serving any obvious purpose. It doesn't get turned on to make proteins and enzymes. We call it junk because it's completely superfluous."

"And what's wrong with my junk DNA?" Van asked impatiently.

"Simply put, we can use junk DNA to identify similarities between people. Each of us has a similarity to each other, and we can ultimately trace back to common ancestors. We can't do that with you. You're one of a kind. You may be incredibly valuable to science."

"Well it's pleasing to know I have some value," commented Van, "even if it's only to science." Hostility hung in the air, and Van was again pacing around his cell like a caged animal.

Lindberg broke it with a smile. "I have a proposal for you, Van, if you're interested." The boy stopped pacing, granting Lindberg his full attention.

"My father was Aaron Lindberg, winner of the Nobel Prize for genetic research." Noting Van's confusion, Lindberg explained, "It's something that started when Earth was our only planet, and we kept it up when we spread out into space. It's the highest honour a scientist can win. It marks them out among the very top of their field. It means fame, immortality." He gave a slightly embarrassed cough, "and quite a lot of money, too. My father recognized that our junk DNA contains a legacy of the creatures that came before us on evolution's ladder. He devised a program to identify and recover those records and recreate some of those creatures. I actually helped him with the

31

program," Lindberg smiled at the thought, "but not nearly enough to win a share of the prize."

"And your proposal?" queried Van.

"I'd like to do something similar with your DNA, Van. I think there are creatures in your past that were not in ours. It is even possible that your ancestors may have crawled from a different primeval sea. The records will be in your DNA, and I'd like to decode them, maybe eventually recreate some of those earlier creatures."

Laurel exhaled slowly. This was big stuff.

"Yes," Van mused, seriously. "I see it now. I've been brainwashed, travelling unconscious for decades in an unmarked ship, and am now stuck in a medical prison in a solar system in the remotest end of the galaxy. Sure, my first priority is to get you your Nobel Prize."

Lindberg maintained his composure. Laurel could tell he had big hopes resting on this. "But just think, Van. We will be finding out who you are, who your ancestors were."

"With respect, Dr Lindberg, I don't even know who my parents are. Let's leave unearthing my reptilian ancestors for another day." Van paused, and Laurel reflected that his outburst was scarcely 'with respect'. A bitter expression crossed Van's face. "I suppose I don't have much choice, anyway? You've already got my DNA to do with what you like."

"No, Van. We abolished slavery a long time ago. Nobody owns you but yourself. You would have to agree."

"And if I say no?" Van's question was decidedly aggressive.

"Then it's no," replied Lindberg evenly.

"I do say no." Van looked defiant. Lindberg sighed.

"Then it doesn't happen." He shrugged.

Laurel could sense strong disappointment in his voice. It was very ungrateful of Van, given it would cost him nothing. There was something rather unpleasant about his general truculence. Dr Lindberg was a very eminent man who had shown great kindness to Van, and Laurel felt he was entitled to some respect. It seemed to her that the boy was unwilling to defer to any kind of authority. Whatever it was in his past that had formed his character could not have been pleasant.

"There's a little more your body tells us," Lindberg said, distracted. "There's scar tissue all over your body, internal and external, which has built up over time. I don't know what you've been up to, but it seems to have been pretty dangerous. You've been in harm's way quite a few times."

Van took this in thoughtfully, and Laurel saw him unconsciously rub a hand on the back of his shoulder. She guessed that he might be fingering one of his scars. He might have an attitude problem, but who knows what he might have been through? Even beyond his dark skin and bright amber eyes, he was exotic. A boy with no past; a boy from nowhere; a dark visitor who came in out of the night.

Lindberg cut in on her thoughts. "I'd be much obliged, Van, if you'd agree to stay in the isolation unit for a time." The boy's scowl flashed back.

"Why?"

"Because I want to be sure about a few things. You've got some bugs inside you; friendly bugs. We all do, but yours are different bugs. And I'm sure you carry immunities like we do, but maybe different immunities. Do me a favour and stay here while we run more tests. It shouldn't take more than a day, maybe two." Lindberg phrased it as a request, and Van evidently decided not to test whether it was, in fact, an order. He nodded reluctantly, and Lindberg made his excuses and left.

Laurel felt awkward being alone with Van for the first time. Polite small talk did not seem appropriate somehow. It was Van who opened the conversation, however. He was much more open now that Lindberg had left.

"You can't imagine how lost I feel, knowing so little in a universe so huge," he said, revealing more of his pain than Laurel had expected.

She smiled, "I know what you mean. I've been fascinated by the universe my entire life, yet after fourteen years I still don't feel I've scratched the surface of what there is to know. Every day I learn something extraordinary about the most ordinary of things."

"You sound like an enthusiast." Van gestured out of the window, "And I don't even know the name of that planet out there."

Laurel couldn't avoid laughing, "Believe me, I learned all there is to know about Akron years ago, and its name is pretty much the only thing I like. That's why I came to live up here. I get to visit every ship that docks, and chat with every crew."

"Could you teach me about the universe? I mean, about different stars and planets, about different cultures?" He looked almost childishly earnest. Laurel smiled inwardly. Oh yes. She could do that. She had soaked up this kind of information like a sponge. She smiled straight into those magnetic eyes, and was rewarded by a shy smile in return.

"Where shall I begin?" she asked.

* * * * *

It took two days. She visited him in the isolation unit during her breaks and whenever she could sneak out of work. He was a model student, listening attentively and retaining everything. Occasionally he asked questions, always intelligent and pertinent.

His face lit up as she told him about the planets she had heard of, from baking worlds decked with pools of liquid sulphur, to ice-worlds gripped in perpetual blizzards, to water worlds where seemingly bottomless oceans teemed with alien life. He sat enthralled as she recounted the exotic life forms of dozens of worlds, and told of places where vegetation floated on clouds. He drank it all in eagerly.

Laurel couldn't remember enjoying herself so much. In talking about it she was experiencing at second hand what she so desperately wanted to taste directly. One day she would, but for now it was alive in her mind. Van, for his part, lapped it up, eager to fill the vacant spaces in his memory. She taught him how to access the library, and whilst she was away he would read up on the information she didn't know. He rapidly soaked up information on the physics of stars and quantum space, to a level of detail she herself found impenetrable beyond the basic facts she needed to get by.

There was none of the anger and impatience Van had shown towards Dr Lindberg, and the two developed the start of a good friendship. Laurel observed that Van's antipathy was only directed at those who held any position of authority and, since she did not, he treated her well. She wondered what it was in his past which made him so completely hostile and unreasonable to people in positions of power, but of course Van knew as little as she did. He agreed to try to keep his mood swings in check.

Van had enjoyed flying most of all. Laurel took him to the simulator during one of her breaks, and they soon discovered that his flying skills must have remained in his memory the same way as walking and talking. It took just a few minutes for Van to get up to speed, after which he sent the simulator spinning and wheeling through virtual space – exploring for many miles the space above the pre-programmed landing lesson. Although it was merely a simulation, Laurel still came out of the machine dizzy and nauseous. It would take her a whole lifetime of learning to become as a good a flyer as Van.

Towards the end of the second day, Dr Lindberg appeared on the isolation unit's screen to announce that Van had a clean bill of health. He could leave the unit and move about the station. With his newfound freedom, their first stop was the recreational park, with which Van fell immediately in love.

"I had no idea it would smell so good." He removed his shoes and planted his bare feet in the lawn, sighing with pleasure at the cool crispness of the grass. Laurel guided him around the park, pointing out the different types of shrub and flower, and Van inhaled deeply from every one. Finally, they lay down in the middle of the park and stared up past the tree branches into space, where Akron hung on its eternal backdrop of stars.

"Okay, now I feel I know nothing about the universe," he laughed. "It's huge."

Laurel laughed. They lay there for almost an hour in silence, watching the universe slowly rotate above them, until it was finally time for Laurel to go to work. Van seemed almost sad. He looked earnestly at Laurel.

"I hope we'll carry on meeting, and you'll tell me more about the universe."

Laurel laughed. "I'm not sure I know much more, but we'll certainly keep meeting if you want to." Van stared at her. Laurel was beginning to learn how to read those strange eyes, and she guessed he was reaching a decision. He was.

"You've told me everything you know, but I haven't told you everything I know."

Laurel stiffened. This sounded like a confession.

"I told you my name is Van. I don't know how I know that, but I do. There's one other thing I know, and I don't know how I know that either."

"What else do you know?" Laurel asked him quietly. Van hesitated.

"I know that something is going to happen. It always does."

4. Tomb-raider

"Perhaps this is our trouble." Blake pointed to a blip on one of the display boards. Laurel stared at it. It was an incoming ship, and a fast one.

"Is it headed here?" she enquired. Blake shook his head.

"No. Close by, but its course takes it directly into orbit round Akron."

Everyone had agreed that if "something was going to happen," it probably meant trouble. Van had readily agreed that his disclosure to Laurel could be passed on, but he was unable to provide anything else. He had endured an afternoon of questioning by the senior station staff, but his wiped memory and hostility to authority meant this was effectively an afternoon wasted.

As the only one to have earned Van's trust, Laurel had been invited to a meeting to help assess the situation. It rapidly become clear that, yet again, the only thing they knew was that they didn't know anything.

"It has to mean trouble," Lindberg declared, but Benson wasn't so sure. As a scientist he didn't like committing himself on such flimsy evidence.

"Let's face it, we don't have much to go on. It really only comes down to a mere vague feeling on Van's part."

"But he's so sure of it," Laurel interjected, "whatever it is, it's going to be big. And he told me because he wanted to help." Benson was still dubious.

"The only other thing he's sure of is that his name is Van, and we don't even know if that's true. Why do you think it means trouble, Lindberg?"

"I think it means trouble because I think *he* means trouble," Lindberg answered. "He's certainly been through enough of it. The scars on his body tell us that. And why should anyone wipe his memory and the ship's log unless there's something to hide?"

Eventually the consensus was for extra vigilance and extra security. As Benson pointed out, there was no harm done, even if nothing did happen.

"I want the first sign of anything unusual," Benson had insisted. "Monitor everything, question everything. Even the apparently routine. Let's run systems checks on everything."

It was because of this that Blake decided to take daily scans at extreme range, and saw the blip well ahead of time. A small, fast-moving ship entering the system unannounced.

"What type of ship?" Dr Benson asked when the news was relayed to him.

"It's very fast," Blake reported. "Could be a courier, or state-of-the-art space yacht. It could even be a military ship." Benson's eyebrows shot up.

"I want to know the moment it comes close enough for a transponder signal to identify it. Keep me posted."

Laurel kept track of the status board over the course of the next day as the ominous blip made its steady progress towards them. If it were indeed trouble, it was coming in fast. There was a certain anxiety among those who had been briefed on Van's warning. Although some feared the approaching ship was coming to destroy the station, Laurel was more fearful that the ship might be targeting Van. Some bounty hunter, or even assassin. Who knew who might be interested in their visitor?

Eventually, the blip flashed as its transponder came within range of the station, and a stream of data lit up the side screen.

"I'm on to it," said Blake as he hurriedly ran his finger down the list of specifications. He began calling out information.

"It's a class C space yacht, equipped with the latest quantum drive, crew of ten, name of *Lodestar.*" He looked up. "That sound familiar?" Laurel shook her head.

"Let's find out who she's registered to," she said as she punched in the yacht's serial number and waited for the result. When it came she let out a long, slow whistle.

"It's Jason Tremayne." Laurel glanced up, shocked. "Tomb-raider Tremayne."

"Now what do you suppose he wants out here?"

Laurel didn't know. "Maybe he's out shopping?" she suggested. Blake smiled. Tremayne was rich, so rich he could buy the whole Auriga system with his pocket change. How he'd acquired that wealth was part legend, part speculation, but honesty and straight dealing didn't feature in many of the stories. Why he should come somewhere so remote was puzzling, Laurel reflected. Men like Tremayne rarely strayed from the overpopulated party planets nearer the centre of the galaxy.

Laurel ran a detailed search on Tremayne while Blake was briefing Dr Benson. As she had suspected, there was plenty to find. He was what the media called an 'aggressive' business dealer, which Laurel assumed was a polite way of saying 'gangster'. Nothing had ever been pinned on him, although his unauthorized biography was entitled 'No Convictions', which Laurel guessed had a double meaning: not only had Tremayne evaded being found guilty and sentenced to anything, but that he didn't believe in anything either, and was completely unrestrained by any moral beliefs. Further research revealed that Tremayne had tried to suppress the biography through the courts, and had hounded and persecuted the author. Laurel looked up from her research. This was someone she did not want to come up against.

Dr Benson entered the room, followed by a worried-looking Blake. Benson was puzzled by the commotion. "Who is this Tremayne character?"

Laurel told him everything she had found, and added "Tomb Raider Tremayne is not the type to make social calls. He could easily be the 'something' we're looking for."

"What do you mean, 'Tomb Raider' Tremayne?"

"It's his nickname. He's a private collector of ancient artefacts, with a museum larger than many planets have. He's quite the connoisseur, and although he's rich enough to buy whatever he wants... well, people are not always willing to sell their heritage. He's not very scrupulous about how he gets what he wants. He loots burial chambers, raids temples, smuggles artefacts... and once he has something, no one else ever sees it. He sits alone in his museum, drinking Scythian champagne and gloating over his collection."

"How do you know all this, Laurel?"

"My parents are archaeologists, sir. On Akron. When I was growing up, he was the bogeyman."

"Not a very pleasant fellow, is he?" mused Benson. "I can imagine better guests to have at the station. Send a hailing signal immediately. I want to know what he wants."

Tremayne was in no hurry to answer. It was fully half an hour before he deigned to acknowledge the station's signal and send them a return signal. Benson had Blake put it up on the big screen so everyone could see what was going on. There were his trademark grey bushy eyebrows and the thick, soft grey hair. His skin seemed to glow with vitality. He was slim, and Laurel noticed that when he moved it was gracefully and with economy. He might have a thug's reputation, but he had a gentleman's manner. The biography had spoken of his "exquisite tastes in food, drink and clothes, too", and Laurel could see this reflected in his immaculate suit.

"Yes?" Tremayne asked, distracted. "Is there something you need?" His expression looked slightly bored, as though the station was of little significance to him and his business.   In truth, he *was* bored, and not a little irritated by their intrusion.

"Welcome *Lodestar*," replied Benson. "We look forward to having you aboard."

Tremayne glanced up with pained surprise. "Ah. The Head of Engineering himself, I see. To what do I owe this magnificent honour?" His tone was clearly sarcastic. "I'm afraid you won't have the pleasure of my company. We are heading direct to Akron itself."

"With due respect, sir, all ships must be cleared here first. We've got to clear you for quarantine, security and smuggling."

"Well that's awfully kind," Tremayne drawled, although his manner implied he was more intrigued by the state of his fingernails than Dr Benson. "But the ship has already been cleared. Competently."

Blake called up the manifest on the *Lodestar* and was astounded to find that it had indeed been pre-cleared. This was unheard of. Tremayne sneered back from the screen. He was used to doing things the way he wanted.

"May I ask the purpose of your visit?" Benson asked.

Tremayne looked up and Laurel saw a quick flash of irritation.

"Pleasure," he said. "I'm looking up an old friend."

"You have friends on Akron?" Benson asked him, surprise in his voice.

"I have friends everywhere," Tremayne replied. Innocent though the remark was, Laurel couldn't help sensing an undercurrent of menace. This man was dangerous.

"Now, if you've finished with your thorough interrogation?" Tremayne cut his transmission without awaiting a response.

Dr Benson fell into his chair and mopped his brow. He had limited experience of diplomacy, and Tremayne had been anything but diplomatic.

"This could be it," Laurel volunteered. "The thing that's going to happen."

Benson's brow furrowed. "We can't be sure that anything *is* going to happen. That's just a feeling Van has. And I can't for the life of me see any connection between Van and a millionaire playboy."

"A dangerous millionaire playboy," Laurel responded, "and one who probably means trouble."

"I suggest we don't worry too much about forebodings," Dr Benson suggested. "Even if this isn't what Van meant, Tremayne is bad news anyway. We need to know what he's planning to do. We can guess it's not good, whatever else it is." Everyone nodded, Laurel included, though she privately felt Van's warning was worth listening to.

Suddenly an idea popped into her head. It was something her parents had been working on. If she were right it meant bad news.

"I know which friend Tremayne is going to visit," she said aloud. Everyone turned towards her.

"Who is it?" asked Blake.

"It's not a who, it's a what. It's the Torquada."

There was a hubbub as everyone started to speak. Benson held up a hand for silence. "Go on," he indicated.

4. TOMB-RAIDER

"Think about it. Akron is a poorly populated rock in the middle of nowhere.

No-one would bother with it except for its ancient civilisation. That's the only reason it attracts top research scientists. Its only artefact of any value is the Torquada. He must have come to add the Torquada to his collection."

Blake looked appalled. "Even he's not that big, or that greedy. The Torquada is Akron's only link with the ancients. It doesn't belong to any individual, it belongs to the planet. He wouldn't be allowed to take it."

"That's never stopped him before," observed Laurel.

"Would someone tell me what this is about?" Dr Benson cut in. He hadn't been brought up on Akron, and engineering was his field, not archaeology. Laurel gave him a quick explanation.

"Akron's original inhabitants died out about a million years ago, long before humans settled the planets. They didn't leave much behind, in fact all that survived is the remains of a temple and one statue."

"A very famous statue," added Blake.

"It represents some ancient god?" Benson asked.

"Not really," Laurel told him. Her father had been telling her about the Torquada for as long as she could remember. He had been there as a boy when it was first discovered in its submerged temple, and had dedicated the rest of his life to excavating the site and learning more about the Akronites. "It was one of three graces, the only one to survive. One was supposed to bring foresight, another brought insight, and the third one, the Torquada, brought harmony."

She fiddled with the controls and brought a picture of it up on screen. Dr Benson stared at the grotesque shape. If anything it looked like a giant roosting bat, upside down and with wings folded. His brain sought out features he could recognise – eyes, nose, mouth – but the mysterious form was impossible to comprehend, strange and unsettling.

"Ugly brute, isn't it? Why would anyone want that?"

Laurel shot him a quick flash of disapproval. "It's not ugly. It's alien. And Tremayne wants it because it's one of a kind. I bet he's come to steal it."

"It's not possible," Blake said. "Take the Torquada? It's been there for a million years."

"He got away with the ruby stone of Trellix IV," observed Laurel, "even with half the galaxy after him."

"He's not got away with it yet," Blake countered. "There are still charges against him in at least three jurisdictions."

"Yes," commented Laurel, "as there have been for ten years. And while his lawyers argue, the ruby stone remains in his collection."

Dr Benson clapped his hands. "Enough talking. Whatever Tremayne is planning, we need to alert the authorities on Akron, including the museum. They need to be prepared."

Blake turned to Laurel. "It looks as though Van was right. Something is happening, just like he said it would."

* * * * *

Laurel called her parents as soon as she got back to her quarters. Although grateful she had taken the trouble to warn them, they plainly thought she was overrating the danger. Her father was slightly dismissive, whilst her mother was more concerned that she was eating well, and wanted to know when Laurel would next be coming home.

"I'm sure the Torquada is safe, dear," her father had said, "It's lasted a million years of turbulent history, I'm sure it can take one more little crisis in its stride."

Laurel tried to explain that Tremayne wasn't just another little crisis. Her parents, of all people, should have known to take him seriously. Laurel could see that they looked down on him without quite understanding that even people you looked down on could outsmart you. They were scholars who treasured precious artefacts for the knowledge they brought. They seemed unable to understand that someone might be motivated by simple greed. Their heads were so far in the clouds, thought Laurel, that they didn't notice the rats at their feet.

It was with misgivings that she ended the conversation with the usual pleasantries.

The next day, she and Van were lying in their now habitual place in the park, watching the shadow of night creep across the face of Akron. Somewhere out there, Laurel thought, are Tremayne and the Torquada. Suddenly they seemed so small, the fate of the statue almost insignificant in the vastness of space. She shook away the thought.

"Do you think the Torquada could be the thing you thought would happen?" she asked.

He frowned. "I don't know. It will definitely be something big."

"This is big," Laurel remarked. "The Torquada is the most significant thing on Akron. It's the planet's only link with its past. There'll be an almighty outrage if Tremayne has come to steal it. There could even be a shooting match."

The dark eyebrows lifted above the amber eyes, but Van made no comment. Laurel remembered the scars on his body. Perhaps he'd seen more than his fair share of shooting matches, even if he didn't remember them.

Any further thoughts were cut short by the arrival of an excited Blake.

"I thought I'd find you here. Guess what? I'm making a trip to Akron." Laurel looked up immediately. She felt immensely jealous. Much as she loved living on the station, Akron was her home and she was tired of only ever seeing it from space. She felt a little guilty for being jealous, though. He had family and friends on Akron too.

She sat up and smiled. "What drags you down there?" she asked brightly, hiding any mean thoughts.

"They want me to beef up security systems in the museum, in case Tremayne has any ideas about lifting the Torquada by stealth. Trivial stuff like trip wires and infra-red beams, but I can't do it from up here. And I got a message from the Deep Lab, so I may as well combine visits. They've got something to show me." He stopped and smiled. "But I saved the best bit till last. Do you want to tag along?"

Laurel gasped. Did she want to come? She leapt up from the grass and threw her arms around Blake. "Yes! Yes, yes, yes!"

"I'll take that as a yes, shall I?" he asked, mischievously.

Laurel laughed, and then realised what she was doing and let go of Blake. He was blushing and looked rather sheepish. She caught a flash of something on Van's face too – something of the wolf about him.

"Fine, we're leaving tomorrow."

Laurel gathered her things from the ground, "I'd best go pack." She caught Blake's expression. "Yes, I know. Ten kilos max."

Much as she loved Akron itself, it also meant a shuttle ride and, if she was lucky, they might let her have a go at the controls herself. She made a quick goodbye to Van, then rushed off to her quarters to prepare.

Van watched Laurel retreat through the park, then lay back again and turned his amber eyes on Akron.

5. Flashes in water

As Laurel had hoped, she was allowed her to take the shuttle controls briefly during their flight down to the planet. It wasn't the most spectacular of tasks – she merely had to follow a calculated trajectory, and this part of the journey was normally handled by the autopilot anyway – but it was good practice. Her formal flight training wouldn't begin for another year, but she spent a few hours each week practising in the station's simulator. When her training started she wanted to be ready.

"Why's it called Deep Lab?" she asked Blake, as she held the controls and watched a schematic of their projected route.

"Well, you see, it's so awfully *deep*," he replied gravely. Laurel glanced at him sharply to see if he was teasing her. He beamed back.

"Shut up!" she laughed.

Blake gave a wince. "Watch where you're going, Laurel," he said with mock-sincerity.

"Blake, we're four hundred miles above the planet. The nearest obstacle *is* the planet. Tell me about Deep Lab."

"Its main instrument is underground. They sealed off some of the giant caves under Akron and flooded them. Now the water acts as a gigantic measuring vat," he told her.

47

"Measuring what?" she asked.

"Radiation. The water traps some of the particles from deep space so they can be recorded," explained Blake. Laurel shrugged. Deep Lab sounded out of her depth.

She concentrated instead on the planet below them, which grew larger with each passing hour. Soon it filled the entire overhead view, and she returned the controls to autopilot. Together, she and Blake spent the remaining time seeking out places they had known on Akron. They soon found their homes and school, and Laurel could also made out the mountain she had conquered on her first climb. It looked so tiny from above, barely a bump, but it had seemed so massive then. Blake pointed to the rift valley, where he and his parents had been travelling the previous year.

Laurel looked over the settlements and small towns to where the ruins of the ancient temple would be, where the Torquada was displayed and still visited by those who sought harmony in their lives. The shuttle was still too high for her to make out the site, but she knew it was there.

The shuttle's entry into the planet's atmosphere was smooth and uneventful, as it always was on automatic pilot, but there was still a powerful tremor as the shuttle's force-field kept the fiery plasma stream kept at bay. It was what Laurel imagined it must be like to plunge through the outer layers of a star. There were ships which could do that, but even Laurel's longing for the exotic and exciting wonders of space had never extended that far.

They arrived just as Auriga's evening rays turned the distant mountains pink. Laurel and Blake laughed as they made their first few hesitant steps on the planet. The station's small artificial gravity field meant that there was a gravity gradient, such that you could sense the difference between its force at your head and your feet. On the planet there was no such gradient, so it took them a few minutes to adjust to the change.

The first night home there were parents and friends. Her mother and father welcomed their errant daughter with hugs and kisses and a home-cooked meal. Laurel was surprised at her own emotions. She'd prided herself on her independence, but the warmth of their greeting reminded her of the deep bond she shared with them. A fleeting wisp of regret flickered through her at the memory of what she'd had to give up. She knew she'd made the right decision, but it had meant abandoning the comfort and security she always felt in their presence. Now, for an evening, they recaptured that closeness and savoured it.

Her parents knew she would want time with her friends, too, and graciously backed out of the home-coming party at an early stage. They were the sort who valued an early bed anyway.

Laurel soon lost any regret that she no longer lived here. While she valued the friends she had left behind, she was no longer part of their world, nor they of hers. Their conversation was about gossip and school events; hers was about travellers from distant worlds, of freighters packed with exotic cargoes, and of Van, the amber-eyed boy who had arrived from nowhere in a ship that was unable to answer its own dark mysteries.

The next morning, her father agreed to take Blake to the temple to beef up the security system. Her father may not have believed the threat Tremayne posed, but did not object to making the temple more secure. Out of interest Laurel tagged along, to watch. To her eye the 'temple' looked more like a few shallow trenches dug on the ground outside a small cave, however she knew the temple was significant. It was home to the only relic of the long-dead Akronian civilization.

Laurel shivered as she stepped into the cave and found herself beneath the gaze of the Torquada, just as she had when her father first brought her here as a child. Although she had criticized Dr Benson, he had been right about one thing: it was hideous. The light from the mouth of the cave played upon it, sending grotesque shadows onto the cave walls beyond it, and highlighting the folds in what archaeologists guessed were wings. Laurel wondered what kind of creature it might represent. With no other information about the long-dead

49

Akronians it was unlikely they would ever unlock the mystery of the statue, but this did not stop all who gazed upon it from wondering. Had there been creatures like this on Akron? Or was it, like the Egyptian Sphinx of the Earth's desert people, a mythical mix of other animals? She was startled by a voice from behind her.

"What harmony do you seek?" She looked round to see the museum curator, the leathery-faced old man who looked after the site. She had met him many times before, whenever her parents brought her to see the Torquada. She recovered from her surprise and greeted him.

"Not exactly," she replied. "But what does harmony mean anyway?"

"I suppose it means balance," the old man told her. "The first of the graces brought foresight. In its presence people would become wise about the future. The second one, insight, made people better able to understand the world." He glanced up at the relic, "And this, the only one which remains, is supposed to bring a sense of proportion to our lives."

"Does it work?" Laurel wondered.

"It works for those who will let it. It works for me because I'm old enough not to seek excitement in my life. I doubt it will work for you. You are not at an age when harmony matters, but it will one day."

Laurel nodded. It was true. It wasn't harmony she sought, but adventure and achievement. Balance could come later, when there was something to balance.

"Pity it isn't foresight," she told the curator. "It would be useful to know Tremayne's plans in advance. But we're doing what we can."

"If what you say is true," her father said as he entered the temple, "I doubt if a few additional alarms will deter a man like Tremayne." He paused and briefly knelt, head bowed, before the statue. There was nothing religious about this, Laurel knew.

5. FLASHES IN WATER

He was not worshipping the statue, he was showing respect to the dead Akronians.

"He has taken jewels from under the nose of royalty, smuggled an entire palace past the eyes of the guards. If he wants the Torquada he will get it. Let us just hope that he does not."

Privately Laurel suspected the same. She had seen the extra touches Blake was putting into the security system, and was not impressed. Tremayne would blow them away with amused contempt. However, she stood up for her friend.

"Blake is very talented," she said, "and if anyone can protect the Torquada, he can." The elderly curator shook his head sadly.

"Greed is a terrible thing. It can overrule our better selves. What this man Tremayne needs is balance." He looked up again at the statue. "May you bring harmony to his life, sweet grace, as you have to mine."

Laurel made her excuses and left, convinced it would take more than a pious prayer to turn the infamous tomb-raider from his path.

As she and Blake drove to the Deep Lab later that afternoon, she confided her misgivings to Blake. She was surprised to find he agreed.

"If Tremayne wants it, he'll get it. He's that sort of man," Blake said. "The extra security might delay him until help can arrive, and it should warn us when he makes his move. But the real stuff I did is hidden. I put a tracker in the statue itself. It won't transmit until we beam a signal at it, so he won't be able to detect it. Wherever he takes it in the galaxy we'll be able to find it. And what's stolen once can be stolen back."

Laurel nodded. She was impressed. That was clever, and Tremayne wouldn't expect it.

* * * * *

Laurel's eyes strained in the near darkness as she peered through the thick round window into one of the giant tanks.

51

There was a flash beyond the glass, and a pinging sound from the loudspeaker on the wall. Then another, then another. Flash, flash, ping, ping. Each flash briefly lit up the ancient subterranean cave, the half-formed stalactites and stalagmites lurking like giant lumbering sea creatures.

Deep Lab was indeed awfully deep. They had taken an elevator down into what felt like the bowels of the planet. As they stepped out Laurel caught the damp reek that hung in the air. She had been caving in Akron's subterranean systems before, and they all smelt like this. There was something else, however. She hadn't expected, so deep inside Akron, to detect the now homely oily smell of the space station; deep down in these caves the scientists had built a lab of steel and glass. Corridors stretched off from the room where they stood, into the darkness beyond, huge windows looking out into the vast dark tanks.

"We call it the aquarium," a smiling white-coated young man told her, "and our colleagues call us the aquanauts."

Blake laughed. "Actually they call you the aqua-nuts." The young man, who Blake introduced as Joseph, laughed in turn.

"I suppose we deserve it," he said. He turned to Laurel. "The big difference is that we're the only marine life allowed anywhere near this particular aquarium," he told her. "Otherwise it's just very clean water, hundreds of thousands of tons of it."

"I'm sure you didn't bring me all this way to look at water," Blake remarked. Joseph looked thoughtful.

"As a matter of fact I did," he replied. He motioned them to come closer to the glass, and turned off the already dim lights. It took a minute or so before their eyes adjusted. Again Laurel's eyes were drawn to the regular golden flashes behind the glass. Flash, ping. Flash, ping.

"It's rather pretty," she remarked. In the reflected light of the flashes she could see Joseph look surprised.

"Yes, I suppose so. I've never thought about it."

5. FLASHES IN WATER

It was fascinating. Flash, ping. Flash, ping. "What is it?" she asked.

"Neutrinos?" guessed Blake. Joseph confirmed it.

"Yes, though you're watching the effects, not the actual neutrinos." Catching Laurel's look, Joseph explained, "Tiny subatomic particles. They come from outer space and pass right through things like planets. We put this water here, and as they pass through one occasionally happens to hit an atom in a molecule of water. We detect the collision and magnify it as a flash and a sound so we can keep track of them."

"Very impressive," observed Blake. "And if you know what fraction of them hit a water atom on their way through, you can multiply up to find how many are coming in."

"Exactly. It may be nothing significant," Joseph said, "and I wouldn't normally have bothered you with it. But we had that message from the station to report anything unusual or anything new."

"I understand. What is it you wanted to show me?" Blake asked. Joseph pointed to the tank.

"Look at it."

Laurel looked. There was a regular flashing deep within it, and a ping on the speaker for each one. Flash, ping. Flash, ping. It was almost hypnotic.

"What are we supposed to be looking at?" asked Blake.

"The frequency," answered Joseph. His face took on a rather grave expression. "Until a week ago we were getting roughly one flash and ping a week. Now look at it."

"One a week!" Blake looked shocked. He stared back into the tank. Laurel did, too. Flash. Ping. Flash, ping.

"What does it mean?" she asked Joseph. He shrugged.

"I don't know. Something's happening, but I don't know what." He turned to Blake. "It's increasing, too. Every day there are more flashes and more pings. Something is pumping out neutrinos at an ever faster rate." Blake looked puzzled, then his face became serious.

"Thanks for this, Joseph. I'll see if we can work out what's happening."

As they rode in the elevator back to the surface, Laurel couldn't help dwelling on Joseph's word, "Something's happening, but I don't know what." It was strangely reminiscent of Van's words, "I know that something is going to happen. It always does."

* * * * *

Shortly after arriving on Akron, Laurel found herself bidding farewell to her parents again, and returning to the base. It wasn't until her fourth shift that she realised she hadn't seen Van since her return. She checked his usual haunts – the park, his quarters in the civilian hostel, the staff canteen – and finally turned to Dr Benson for help.

"The boy has an attitude problem," Dr Benson told Laurel, his face glowering with suppressed anger. "He's a danger to both himself and the base."

Van, she was told, was back in his isolation unit, in a state of heightened security.

"He's completely incapable of respecting any rules or authority. I'm sure that was fine when he's all alone on that ship of his, but we have several hundred lives to think about up here, and we can't let him put them at risk just because he doesn't know how to follow instructions." Dr Benson's face was awash with an equal mix of disappointment and rage as he paced anxiously around his office. No one could argue he hadn't given Van a fair chance, Laurel reflected.

"But what did he do?" she asked.

"He tried to take his ship out. No permission, no clearance, no safety procedures. He just felt like a day trip so off he sets. Of course, the alarm sounded when he attempted to open the outer doors of the docking bay, and we caught him before he boarded. He went berserk, mind. It took three men to hold him down."

"But still, it's his ship. He didn't mean any harm."

"Mean no harm? No. But as it happens a freighter was docking at the time. Had he managed to leave he would undoubtedly have caused a collision and, most likely, damage to the entire station." Dr Benson sat down at his desk. "Lives are at risk, Cadet Mackay. We can't just do as we please and forget the rest."

"Have you asked him what he was doing?" she asked.

"We didn't need to. It was obvious. He just raved when we caught him. For now we're keeping him in confinement until his behaviour improves." Benson looked her in the eye.

"Frankly, Laurel, I would not be surprised if Van is the 'thing' that is going to happen. It fits perfectly. Until we know why he is here, and what his intentions are, there is no way we can allow him the freedom of the station, let alone permit him to take his ship out of dock."

"I apologise on his behalf, Dr Benson. May I see him?"

"Yes, please do. He seems to get on better with you than anyone else. Perhaps you can get sense into his skull."

It was a very sullen and subdued Van she confronted in the isolation unit. There was a bruise on his forehead, and a small cut just above one eyebrow. Clearly he hadn't given in without a fight. The hardback chair had been removed from the cell – presumably in case he wished to use it as a weapon – and a containment field had been put in place to keep him under control. Laurel couldn't even go to comfort him.

"What were you thinking, Van?"

"I was leaving. I foolishly thought nobody owned anybody any more, and that I could make my own choices. But that was just words. The moment I tried to do anything by myself, they stopped me. If you don't have slavery, then what is this?" As he spoke he threw himself against the containment field. It flashed and hummed as it repelled him back across the room.

"Van, it's to stop you doing harm either to yourself or the rest of us."

"I just wanted to leave," he said wearily, sinking into the corner of the room.

"Why? I thought you liked it here? I thought you wanted to find out more about yourself. Why leave now?" Laurel saw something quite like despair fill his face.

"Because I'm bad news, Laurel. Something bad is going to happen and it's because of me. My presence here is endangering everyone. I just wanted to get away so that people like you don't get hurt." He looked miserable.

"But why didn't you just tell that to Dr Benson?" she asked, and was startled to see how quickly the anger came back to his face.

"I don't have to ask permission for everything I do," he snapped. "I can make my own decisions."

"We all can," Laurel responded, "but if we're sensible we take advice. I do," she added.

"I just don't like being confined," said Van darkly. Laurel suddenly felt a wave of sympathy for him.

"Van, I think I can get you out of here. Dr Benson doesn't want to keep you locked up forever. He's just annoyed that you did something without thinking about the danger to others." Laurel put on her most pleading look and watched the almost hypnotic amber eyes stare into her own. "I'm going to vouch for you. Promise you'll ask my advice before you do anything and I'll ask Dr Benson to let you out."

With visible reluctance Van eventually agreed. With even more reluctance Dr Benson ultimately did the same. Laurel noticed that although people were polite to herself and Van as they went about the station, there was a new edginess about their reaction to their visitor. Van had clearly forfeited much of the goodwill and sympathy which had greeted his arrival.

There was a distinct coolness about Blake, too. When Van had first appeared she had been conscious of spending less time with Blake as she set about filling some of the gaps in Van's knowledge. Blake had seemed able to deal with that and to understand it. On the trip to Akron they had spent easy hours in each other's company, but since the return to the station, where Van's presence loomed large, Blake was conspicuous by his absence. She rarely saw him, and he did not seem to be seeking her company.

Van took up much of her free time anyway. She filled him in with details about Tremayne's background and history, and noted that Van seemed to take a special interest in him. If Tremayne did make a bid to seize the Torquada and they came up against him, it would be as well to know as much as possible about him.

She also took Van through the details of what they had seen on Akron, both at the temple and later at the Deep Lab. Van was fascinated by her account of the water tank, but had no more idea than she did about what its significance might be. It was Blake who solved that problem.

"Attention," called the speakers. Dr Benson's face appeared on screen. "There's to be a scientific conference in room B5 in half an hour. I need all communications and space science personnel there." The connection was severed abruptly. Laurel was surprised. These conferences were regularly called to discuss new findings or events, but usually with a few days' notice. Half an hour was unprecedented.

Laurel and Van went to B5 immediately. They managed to wheedle Van's admittance on the rather flimsy grounds that his ship counted as 'space science'. Laurel looked around the room. All of the top departmental directors were there, plus most of the media team and a few of the most talented juniors. There must have been thirty people in the room, far more than usual. Blake was sitting at the front, a grave expression on his face.

Something serious was going to be announced, she realised. There was a hush as Dr Benson got to his feet. He cleared his throat nervously.

"I don't yet know what this is about, but Blake tells me it is necessary," Dr Benson announced. Laurel and Van exchanged glances with each other as Blake rose from his seat. He looked across to them without smiling.

"I have been trying to account for the rise in neutrino emissions detected by Deep Lab on Akron. I soon established that their source was the planet's sun, Auriga." Blake paused and pressed a switch to bring up a diagram on screen. It showed the star Auriga with a stream of particles coming out in all directions, some of which were passing through Akron.

"Although the current rate of neutrino emissions is alarmingly high, more worrying is that the rate is actually increasing," Blake went on. "We have no theoretical corollary for the rate of increase in emissions, however I was able to compare the data we have with previous observations. As you can see, there is a characteristic pattern to the rate of increase." Blake indicated a chart on the screen behind him. "I finally tracked down three similar patterns of neutrino emission increase. If you look at the captions below you will see that the stars concerned were Theta Orionid, Delta Crux, and Himmelberg." Benson, sitting two along from Blake, let out a loud gasp of astonishment.

"Yes," said Blake. "As Dr Benson has already spotted, all three of those stars have one more thing in common. They all went nova."

Not for the first time, pandemonium erupted in the auditorium.

6. Calling all ships

Van had been mystified by the panic the announcement had caused, until he and Laurel got back to her quarters and she was able to explain. He sat at her desk, whilst Laurel paced anxiously around the room.

"When a star goes nova, a fundamental balance in its structure is tipped over and the star undergoes a sudden and dramatic increase in brightness and temperature. Effectively the star expands rapidly, forcibly expelling some of its outer layers in the process."

Now it was Van's turn to get up and pace. "This is not good news."

"No!" Laurel laughed anxiously at Van's understatement. "Quite apart from the fact that Akron would most likely be swallowed and destroyed by the expelled outer layers, the entire life support system of the planet is dependent upon a delicate environmental balance. Double the heat output of the sun and Akron becomes uninhabitable."

"That is, if it isn't swallowed up entirely when Auriga goes nova," Van noted. This was terrible news. "So, the question is what do we do about it?"

"No, the question is *can* we do anything about it? I don't think we have many options."

Van suddenly looked thoughtful. The amber eyes slipped out of focus as he followed a thought.

"What is it?" demanded Laurel.

Van stared seriously at her. "I wonder," he mused, "if this is it – the thing that happens. I wonder if whoever built my ship sent me here because they knew the star would go nova? If so, the question is why?"

It was an intriguing thought, but before Laurel could follow it up there was a knock at the door, and Blake poked his head around. Laurel saw him tense as he saw that Van was there, but she motioned him to come in.

"We were just talking about our options," she told him.

"That's easy," Blake grunted. "We run."

"Run?"

"Yes, run. When Auriga goes nova it will incinerate half of the local sector. We're in the wrong half."

Laurel was aghast. "You're talking about tens of thousands of people! The moon settlements, mining operations, not to mention Akron's cities themselves. They can't all run."

Blake was adamant. "They have to. The choice is run or die. It's not a problem for most of the other systems, since they'll have years to do it in. The explosion won't travel above light speed so they'll have time to evacuate everyone. The most pressing problem is for the station and Akron. Auriga could go nova at any point. Everyone is going to have to out-run it until we are far enough away to jump into quantum space. Dr Lindberg is arranging the evacuation now."

"How many people are there on Akron?" asked Van.

"About ten thousand," said Laurel. "How much time do we have?" Blake gave her a weak smile and shrugged helplessly.

"We don't know. There isn't enough data to model that. We just know that it will happen, and we need to get everyone out before it does."

Van looked puzzled. "How can you evacuate ten thousand people?"

* * * * *

It was Dr Lindberg who answered that question at a packed and acrimonious meeting of the station. Laurel was amazed at the turnout. Most of the station's population was there, and the assembly was held rather incongruously in the recreational park, with anxious personnel sitting on the grass or under the trees. A public address system had been hastily rigged so that everyone could hear what was being said and take part in the discussion. In less dramatic circumstances it could have been a picnic or barbecue, Laurel thought. But Dr Lindberg was talking of more serious matters.

"If all cargo is jettisoned, the freighters can manage between 50 and 100 people. The small yachts and messenger ships can take maybe a dozen. If we reckon on an average of maybe 50 per ship, it will take about 200 ships." A huge din broke out, and it took Dr Benson, even more flustered than normal, a few minutes to restore order.

"If I understand what people are saying, Dr Lindberg, we don't have 200 ships, or anything even close to that number," he announced.

"No," Lindberg replied, and before the hubbub could start again added, "but we can get them. I propose we put out an all-points bulletin to every vessel within two days' range. Every ship that flies: cargo freighters, passenger ships, luxury yachts and courier bugs; all of them. We will ask them to dump cargo in holding orbits and make maximum speed to Akron. Meanwhile, we organise the inhabitants for evacuation. Each ship will arrive, fill to capacity with evacuees and leave at maximum speed. I believe, with organisation and cooperation, that we can, if we're lucky, complete the evacuation." He shrugged, then added, "So long as we have enough time, of course." Once again a huge din broke out as everyone clamoured to have their say.

Dr Benson granted the floor to Dr Stevens, a grey-haired figure who was part of the exo-organisms team. Laurel had worked with him before, when the station was infected with a particularly prolific breed of space spores. Then she had quite liked him, but today he was not bidding for popularity.

"Look," Stevens appealed to the crowd, "this is an unreasonable panic reaction. None of us knows whether Auriga is even going to go nova. Can we seriously be planning to evacuate an entire solar system, disrupt all our work and inconvenience hundreds more ships, on the say so of some teenager, based on nothing more than a simple statistical pattern? There is a very small sample, and we haven't even proven a causal link. We must ask ourselves, have any stars shown the same neutrino pattern and not gone nova? Are we going to disrupt all of our work and fly off in a panic because of some very dubious science? We must stay until we get more data."

Laurel could tell, from the murmurs of assent which greeted this short speech, that he had some supporters. She had also seen Blake bristle at the mention of 'some teenager', but it was Lindberg who chose to reply.

"Facts remain facts even when 'some teenager' looks at them, Dr Stevens. Blake may be young, but I am not, and I've checked his data thoroughly." He pointed to Auriga, through the dome above the park. "That star is going to blow."

Laurel was among the many who followed Lindberg's gesture and looked up at the star as he said this. Until now it had always seemed like a familiar friend, the eternal source of light and life. Now she felt quite differently; Auriga hung sinister in the sky, threatening to rain fire and death without warning.

The debate raged backwards and forwards. Stevens had his supporters, but Laurel noticed that most of the senior scientists backed Lindberg's plan, including the entire astrophysics team.

6. CALLING ALL SHIPS

"What about the station itself?" demanded a woman Laurel didn't recognize.

"Non-essential staff will be evacuated along with Akron," Lindberg told her. "The remainder will supervise the evacuation from the station, and then get ourselves out as fast as we can."

"And what of the people on Akron?" inquired Stevens. "I suppose they must all meekly abandon their homes and livelihoods and flee on a whim? What if they don't want to?"

Dr Benson fielded this one. "We will, of course, try to persuade them. And we will aim to evacuate all those that wish to be saved. But this is, after all, a free community. If people elect to stay, then we must leave them to die."

The arguments raged backwards and forwards, with no resolution. Eventually Benson proposed a vote. "A *yes* means we go ahead with the evacuation. A *no* means we wait and collect more data before we act," he declared. There was general assent that this was a fair way to decide. The vote was to be held that evening, with everyone on the station eligible to vote.

Laurel, Van and Blake met later in the canteen to hear the results of the vote. Blake picked at his salad absent-mindedly, anxious about the way things had gone. He was not so convinced that a vote was the best way to solve the impasse.

"The thing about a *no* vote," he told Laurel and Van, "is that it effectively amounts to a death sentence. A lot of people will want to leave the station, but unless we can put out an appeal for ships then there won't be any transport for them." He looked grim.

"You can come on my ship," volunteered Van. "There's plenty of space, although I admit there's no living quarters." Blake looked surprised, and thanked him. Laurel was surprised by this move too. There had been some edginess between Blake and Van ever since she took Van under her wing. She acknowledged she had spent much less time with Blake than she used to, but dismissed the thought. These were unusual times.

The results of the vote were broadcast to the entire ship. Much to the relief of the science teams, nearly three-quarters of the station's personnel had voted for the evacuation. The doubters were outnumbered.

"You've been vindicated," Laurel told Blake. He was clearly pleased, but of course something was still pressing on his mind.

"We won the vote," said Blake. "But now let's see if we can win the race."

* * * * *

Lindberg spent some time working on the mayday message. The message would naturally be received on Akron as well as by nearby ships and trading posts, and so he needed to keep the message sufficiently urgent and direct, whilst avoiding any dramatic details that might cause panic or unrest on the planet.

"CALLING ALL SHIPS WITHIN RANGE OF AKRON. THE PLANET MUST BE EVACUATED IMMEDIATELY. YOUR HELP IS NEEDED. ALL SHIPS NEEDED. PLEASE COME."

It was dramatically effective. Sent on all sub-space frequencies, they didn't have long to wait for a response. Within minutes the communications board lit up as the first replies came in, and they were still flooding in hours later. Ship after ship dumped cargo as requested and headed toward Akron at maximum speed. Only the passenger liners were unable to offer help, as they were already full, though even some of these deposited passengers on the nearest habitable planet and headed out towards the station. Even Tremayne called in from the *Lodestar*, languidly looking at his fingernails as he announced that his ship would play a modest part in the exercise, taking perhaps a dozen evacuees in addition to its crew. It might suit his purposes.

'What impresses me," mused Lindberg as he looked in to see how it was going, "is that we've told everyone about the risk, and not a single one has chosen to stay out of it. They're coming anyway."

Blake was gratified by the scale of the response. "This has to be one of the biggest evacuations in the history of space travel," he exclaimed.

"Indeed," Lindberg told him, and nodded at the screen. "And that is going to be the biggest armada ever assembled in space."

He turned his attention to Akron, the brown and white globe hanging above them. "That, however, is going to be quite a headache."

* * * * *

Just how big a problem Akron was going to be struck Laurel forcibly when she took an incoming call from her mother. The anxious face looked out at her.

"Laurel dear, are you all right? There's been a dreadful alarm about people trying to make us to leave." She looked pale, as so often. Laurel had suggested more than once that a little make-up would improve her complexion, but any such ideas had always been dismissed. Her work was what mattered, she insisted, not her appearance. Now the pallor was compounded with worry.

"No, mother, no-one's going to force anyone to go anywhere. The station has put out an appeal for ships so we can evacuate you all out of the system before Auriga goes nova, but there's no question of force."

Her mother looked taken aback. "Goodness me, Laurel, you're in on it, too. What is going on up there?"

"The star is unstable. Its neutrino decay patterns indicate that the internal structure is reaching a delicate point…" She sighed; she could tell she was losing her mother's attention. She cut to the bare facts, "Auriga is going to explode. When it does, Akron will be consumed in the fire and burned to a cinder. We're hoping to get everyone off the planet before the star goes nova."

"Heavens, dear, any star can go nova. You never know which ones and when. If we worried about that we'd never settle on any planets at all. There's no proof that Auriga is unstable."

"Mother, it's not like that," Laurel explained patiently. "Only a few stars go nova, and Auriga is warning us with its neutrino count. It's going to get very hot very quickly and we all have to be far away by then."

"But it might take years!" her mother exclaimed. "We can't abandon our work here to go haring off into space on the off-chance of it happening. We're making amazing progress with the temple, dear. We can't throw that all away." Laurel realised that her parents were so completely immersed in their work that the archaeology of the Akronians mattered more to them than anything else in the universe. Indeed, she reflected, they probably didn't even notice the rest of the universe.

Her mother paused, sighed again, and spoke frankly. "Your father and I have been talking it over, and we've decided we're not leaving. If it gets hotter we can just shelter in one of the deeper caves until it's all over."

Laurel felt the beginnings of panic rising inside her. Her parents could not stay on that planet. They needed to face up to the reality of the situation, not retreat into a cave in the hope things would get better. She had another, unpleasant thought. If her own parents were so reluctant to face up to the risk, what would the others be like? She had to persuade them.

"No cave is deep enough," she said levelly. "The temperature is going to rise by thousands of degrees. The surface of Akron will be scoured with radiation. No organisms will survive. The atmosphere itself will burn away, leaving a lifeless radioactive hulk – if anything of the planet survives at all."

"Laurel, dear, you've always been prone to exaggerate. This is just propaganda put out by the station to panic us into compliance. Oh, I dare say some of the more alarmist types will head off in your ships, but I've talked around, and I can assure

66

you that most of us are planning to stay put. Akron has survived millions of years, I think it can survive this."

"Akron may well survive, Mother. But everything else will be incinerated. You'll leave no more trace than the ancient Akronians did. You simply must leave. We may not have much time."

Laurel's mother faltered, but her father entered the picture on the screen. His speech was short and effective. "Laurel, this is our home. This is all we have. Nothing will make us leave and we are not talking about this anymore." He reached forwarded and terminated the connection.

Laurel sat before the blank screen, and reflected that her parents were as determined to stay as she was to make them leave. She began to realise what Lindberg meant when he described Akron as one of the biggest problems. They could arrange as many ships as they liked, but an evacuation wouldn't work if the evacuees refused to participate.

Laurel was not in a good mood when she left her quarters to join her shift. As she wandered down the corridors she became aware of the buzz of purposeful activity all around her. Entire teams of people were supervising the ships as they came in, assigning them to holding orbits about the planet. The normally quiet communications room was a hive of activity, people yelling out instructions to each other and to unseen pilots. She took her seat before the status board, now a mass of flashing lights and scrolling data. On her screens, she watched the huge freighters, lining up in distant orbit, jostling for space with the smaller messenger ships. It was a rag-tag armada all right. The total ran into hundreds, with some giant deep space ships circling the planet itself; these were so large they never landed on planets themselves, but were served by a smaller fleet of shuttles.

The scene looked like utter confusion, but she could see the method in it. Each ship had its precise and unique trajectory. She joined in the work and set about calculating landing sequences, assigning ships a time and place for touchdown and take-off. It all had to be planned to a tight, precise schedule or there would be mayhem.

At the end of her shift, Laurel was summoned to Dr Lindberg's office in the command centre. He confirmed her suspicion that, like her parents, many were refusing to evacuate Akron.

"It's proving harder than we expected to convince them. There's a big faction forming of those who refuse to leave." He looked rather weary, thought Laurel, either from the physical and mental effort of co-ordinating so large an enterprise, or perhaps from the frustration of dealing with people who so stubbornly refused to accept reality.

"They have the right to stay, of course," he acknowledged, "but our job is to keep the casualties as low as possible."

"Where do I fit in?" Laurel asked him.

"Cadet Mackay, you're local, you know the people down there. You know how their minds work. And you've been in on this neutrino alert from the very beginning. I want to put together some sort of communications team, and if you're ready to return to that planet down there, I could really use you."

Laurel welcomed the chance to convince her parents and bring them to safety. "Count me in, sir."

"Now, I won't say it may be dangerous. I know that it will be. If the star blows while you're down there, then not you or anyone else on Akron is getting out alive. Also," he looked thoughtful, "I've seen people panic in the face of danger before, and decency doesn't always win out over the survival instinct. They may well fight for a place out. Be careful."

Laurel was sobered by this thought. Her whole life she had craved adventure, but now she was in an adventure of her own she realised the gravity of the situation. Things were going to be nasty.

As she motioned to leave and prepare for the journey, Lindberg hesitated. He clearly had something else to say, and it didn't look like good news.

"One other thing, Cadet Mackay," he said. "I don't know whether you've heard this, but your father has emerged as one of the leaders of the faction resisting evacuation. I don't know if that alters things."

"No, sir, it does not," Laurel replied firmly, but inwardly her heart sank. Her parents were so blind. They always had been, to some degree, but this time it might mean the deaths of thousands. She regained her composure, and held her head high. If she had to fight them as well, then so be it.

7. Harmony

Laurel was not prepared for what she would find on Akron. Back on the station activity had been frantic but structured; orders were issued and acknowledged, decisions were made. Down on Akron the activity was merely frantic. Anxious refugees swarmed around the spaceport with no apparent direction, accosting harassed officials and demanding to know what was happening. The effect was both chaotic and confusing. Laurel's heart sank when she realised that things might become more chaotic as the danger posed by Auriga increased.

Among the hubbub of the spaceport, Laurel overheard the angry voice of a middle-aged woman as she browbeat one of the uniformed spaceport officials.

"Ten kilograms. That's what it says," she insisted, pointing to a sign. "It's always ten kilograms per passenger, so what's this nonsense about taking nothing at all?" The official looked pained. He had clearly had to explain this many times.

"Madam, this is not a holiday cruise, it's an emergency evacuation. We can barely manage to carry all the people as it is, never mind their luggage."

"Well I still demand my ten kilos!" she retorted.

71

"Very well," the official conceded, and the woman preened with triumph. He pointed to a group of children a little further back. "Although, of course, we will have to leave a child behind to die. Would you care to choose? Perhaps the one with brown hair?" The child in question gazed back with wide, innocent eyes.

The woman turned bright red, an uneven combination of both fury and embarrassment. Laurel thought the woman might explode, but she simply turned on her heel and left. Laurel gave a supportive smile to the official, who nodded back in acknowledgement. This was not an easy job.

Laurel continued her journey against the flow of refugees through the spaceport. Untidy groups of families sat around awaiting the call to board their ship, forlornly clutching stray possessions which they still hoped to take with them. She watched as one young family got the call to board their ship, the *Ulysses*. The parents gathered up their children and hurried to the gates, pausing only as they mounted the ramp and realised the haste with which they were leaving behind their homes. The mother turned around to look through the huge window, taking a last look at everything they were abandoning, everything they had known.

Laurel had said goodbye to Akron when she had joined the station, but she had left with optimism and anticipation tempering the sadness of her leaving. The family were leaving behind everything to pursue an uncertain future. The husband put a tender arm around his wife and gently shepherded her and the children through the gate. At least that family would have their lives and each other, Laurel reflected. Those who refused to leave would have neither. Laurel frowned grimly when she realised this might include her parents.

If her parents had been stubborn when she spoke to them from the space station, they were utterly resolved to stay when she confronted them in their own home. She had enjoyed a pleasant home-cooked meal, and they now sat in front of the fireside. After the usual chatter about the day's events, it did not take long for the conversation to turn to the matter of evacuation. Her parents had been reinforcing their plans, and her father remained the most determined.

"Laurel, dear. Blake may be a splendid scientist, but his evidence is flimsy. The universe is full of neutrinos from all kinds of sources. If every neutrino burst meant a nova star, the universe would be exploding all around us."

"But it's the pattern of the neutrino burst that matters. Auriga is following the same pattern as Delta Crux, Theta Orionid and Himmelberg... you've heard what happened there. We need to be light years away when Auriga blows."

"*When* it blows!" laughed her mother. "You mean *if* it blows. Look, Laurel, we've talked this over for hours. We're not giving up our life's work on a whim. By all means, you must go if that is what you want. But when you come back, we'll still be here for you."

And that was that. No amount of reasoning could dissuade them. Laurel would have been irritated if it was merely pig-headedness, but this was suicidal, and more than half the planet took the same view. They seemed to believe that ignoring the problem would make it go away.

She was still fuming half an hour later when a call came through from Blake. She took it in her room to avoid sparking any more arguments with her parents.

"Hey Laurel, how's it going down there?" he asked.

"Chaos!" she said simply. "What have you got?"

"Two pieces of news. Firstly, the *Lodestar* has gone into a descent sequence toward Akron without waiting to be assigned a landing place or time. It looks like Tremayne is making his move. He's going after the Torquada before we can take it out on one of the freighters."

Laurel stiffened. On top of the evacuation, she still had to thwart Tremayne. "Just what I needed! What's the other news?" Blake looked grave.

"It gets worse. Deep Lab have reported that the rate of neutrino collisions is going off the scale. I've checked the patterns and its not good. Auriga could go critical within three days, quite possibly sooner." Blake paused, reflecting on this news. "Laurel, do take care of yourself."

She stared at Blake's familiar face on the communicator screen, hesitant to end the conversation and be returned to the reality of events on Akron.

"You too," she said finally, before closing the connection.

Laurel felt overwhelmed by events. Tremayne was already making his bid to seize the Torquada before it could be taken off-planet, and he had to be stopped. Meanwhile the star was on the verge of going nova with several thousand people yet to be rescued. She also had to help coordinate a planet-wide information broadcast, as well as achieve the impossible by convincing her parents to change their minds and leave Akron. She sighed, and remained at her desk for a few minutes, enjoying the brief calm whilst her mind worked through her options.

She decided she should first go to the temple and warn the curator that Tremayne was on the prowl, and help him to prepare for the unwelcome visitor. Once the Torquada was taken to safety she could focus on the evacuation. She set off straight away, gunning her scooter through the traffic as fast as she could go. There was a huge build-up of vehicles as the thousands who had elected to leave the planet tried to get away as quickly as possible. Most of them were heading in the opposite direction, to the spaceport, and again Laurel found herself fighting against the flow of evacuees. She didn't like to think how hard things might become when she needed to fight her way back to the spaceport.

Laurel's heart sank when she spotted a number of vehicles parked outside the temple. Tremayne must already be here. She moved quietly to the cave entrance. She could hear the faint murmur of voices, and see the flickering of lights and shadows as people moved around inside. She froze as she heard the boom of a familiar voice. Tremayne.

She slipped inside quietly and crouched behind a rock towards the back of the temple, amid the shadows. When she was certain she had not been seen she peered cautiously over the rock. Several figures stood in a pool of light before the Torquada, including Tremayne and the curator. The Tomb Raider's companions were armed, probably some of Tremayne's thugs. Brooding silently in the background, the Torquada seemed more likely to bring bad fortune than harmony. Tremayne was speaking.

"You should look upon us as guardians." Tremayne paced around the pool of light, and smirked as he ventured, "Saviours, perhaps. You cannot deny that the relic would be destroyed if your dear Auriga went nova before you'd taken it off-world. All harmony will be torn apart in the force of the exploding star. We can ensure it is taken away safely." Catching the hostile look on the curator's face, he added, "And of course, to prove our good faith we'll take you along as well, old man. You can gaze into that beautiful face for as long as you live." Tremayne gestured with irony to the relic's hideous face.

"I'm surprised you don't offer me money," remarked the curator, dryly.

"There's money if you want it," Tremayne volunteered readily. "That's the easy part. You can have whatever you want. We can set you up as curator, and you can wallow in comfort as well as harmony." He'd never himself found money to be a problem, but he'd seen others pursue it obsessively.

The curator looked weak standing before Tremayne's thugs, but he remained defiant. "My needs are simple these days. The statue itself has already brought me comfort and harmony."

"Good things should be shared," Tremayne cut in, "and I intend to get some harmony for myself." The curator rewarded him with a sad little smile.

"Oh that you will never get, Mr Tremayne. You can steal the Torquada right now and travel with it from one end of the galaxy to the other, praying before her three times a day. But you'll never find harmony because there is no room for harmony in your life."

Tremayne sneered. "Maybe so. But then, am I acting like a man who seeks harmony?" He reached across to the statue and touched it, as if claiming it. "There's always room for more clutter in my life, and only one person stands in the way of me and the Torquada."

Laurel had listened to enough of Tremayne's bloated speeches.

"Two people!" cried Laurel as she stepped out of hiding into the light. Tremayne's composure never faltered a moment.

"Oh, look. A girl! Well that does change the odds a little," he laughed, motioning pointedly to his five armed men. They stood to attention, their weapons at the ready. Tremayne smiled expansively and turned back to the curator. "Look, we can do this the easy way or the hard way. The easy way is that we take winged beauty here back to my ship, and you and I head off home for a comfortable life and a new adventure. To my way of thinking that's a safe bet. I'm safe. You're safe. And the Torquada is safe. For the life of me, what's wrong with that?" The curator's eyes softened as Tremayne said this. Indeed, it would be safer.

"How about a lack of law and decency?" Laurel shouted across the temple.

"Law and decency?" echoed Tremayne, not in the least upset by Laurel's hostility. He laughed. "Why, I'm Jason Tremayne. My heart has as much room for law and decency as it does harmony!" He motioned to one of this thugs. "Bring the loading equipment, we can get this thing into my ship before sundown and be in quantum space in time for dinner. We leave the curator."

"You can't do this!" Laurel cried.

76

7. HARMONY

"I can't? Oh my!" Tremayne said in a shrill imitation of her voice. "Well, there are only two people in my way."

"Three people," called a voice levelly from the shadows. A figure clad entirely in black stepped from behind the statue. Laurel recognized Van instantly. He moved silently and with an ominous sleekness that reminded Laurel yet again of the tiger. Tremayne remained nonchalant

"So now we have a girl *and* a boy? If they'd had defence like this on Trellix IV I'd never have got the ruby stone."

Van stepped forwards into the circle of light between Tremayne and the Torquada. He stood with his hands behind his back and looked the Tomb Raider in the face. In the dim light of the cave his amber eyes shone wide and bright like glowing embers in the night. Tremayne flinched briefly. This might be dangerous.

"What in the world are you?" he whispered.

Van answered Tremayne in a soft voice. "My name is Van." He leaned forward slightly, putting his weight on to the balls of his feet. He seemed on the verge of pouncing, every inch a predator. "You know, you really should hire more alert bodyguards." Van brought his hand from behind his back to reveal five small, silver power packs. He tossed them on to the sandy floor at Tremayne's feet, where they emitted a brief blue flash of radiation as they landed. Then Van resumed his menacing pose.

For the first time, Laurel saw Tremayne lost for words. He looked sharply at his bodyguards, who struggled with their weapons and confirmed that Van had indeed deactivated them. From the look on Tremayne's face Laurel guessed those guards would not be in his employ much longer. Finally, Tremayne spoke.

"I'm a gambler," he said, "and the key to good gambling is knowing when your opponent is bluffing. Either he holds the cards or he does not, and you have to know which," he paused theatrically to inspect his fingernails. He seemed utterly uninterested, but Laurel was wise enough to suspect he was bluffing himself. "I look at you and I see a boy prepared to take on myself and five bodyguards. Five *unarmed* body guards, I concede," he threw a furious glance at his thugs, "but each of them trained killers. So maybe you have the cards, and maybe you don't."

"So call my bluff," Van suggested softly. In the flickering light, Laurel saw muscles tense beneath his clothing. Tremayne instinctively tensed too, but then relaxed.

"My gambler's instinct tells me that would be the wrong thing to do," he concluded. "I don't feel like paying to look at your cards; at least, not today." Tremayne pulled himself up to his full height, and spoke in loud, measured tones, "But believe me when I say this: I *will* be back, and the Torquada *will* leave this planet on my ship." Tremayne held his head high as he turned to stride out of the temple, but his legs disobeyed and the Tomb Raider found himself collapsed on the floor, scrabbling in the dusty sand. Van approached him with a large, steel knife, its blade shimmering in the uncertain light. Tremayne let out a gasp of alarm.

"A little stealth can be a dangerous thing," Van smiled softly but menacingly, as he reached down towards the Tomb Raider with his knife, to cut free his shoes. Laurel fought to stifle a laugh as she realised that Van had somehow fused his shoes together when he had thrown down the power packs. Tremayne shot him a look charged with pure hatred and then fled the temple, any pretence of dignity lost.

With the bodyguards gone, Laurel breathed an audible sigh of relief, and then raced across the temple to her friend.

"Van! What are you doing here?" she cried as they hugged. Van grinned.

"I guessed you might need some back-up. I think I may have guessed right." The curator was also grateful, and wouldn't stop shaking Van by the hand. Laurel felt the celebrations were premature, however. Despite Tremayne's undignified exit, she knew he would fulfil his final promise: he would indeed return, and did indeed intend to leave with the Torquada on his ship.

Van explained that his ship was in orbit around Akron, and that he had come down to the planet in a shuttle. "No, this time I asked permission, and I'm here with full approval." He laughed, after catching Laurel's anxious look.

"So what now?" he asked.

"Now?" Laurel said, in all seriousness. "Now we save the planet."

* * * * *

Although the planet itself could not be saved, Laurel hoped to save as many of its people as possible. If she had her way she would make the evacuation compulsory. Without too much trouble they could have forcibly removed everyone from the planet and then, after the nova, those who had not wanted to leave would have agreed this had indeed been the correct course. However, this was not possible in a free community, where individuals had the right to choose their own destinies, however foolish those choices might be.

It was decided instead that a debate was the best solution. Each side would put forward their arguments, and everyone could make an informed decision. The broadcast would take the same form as an election debate, with each side allowed six minutes without interruption. Laurel was relieved to see that the moderator was to be Flint Harrison, an elder statesman of Akron's media network. He had been anchoring broadcasts for as long as anyone could remember. He made a point of never revealing his age, and it was said by some that he hadn't been born at all, but had just crawled out of the planet's rocks one day in its ancient past. While very hard and very strict, from which his nickname 'Flint' was derived, he was also scrupulously fair. There would be no one-sided treatment with him in charge.

He went on screen first, his face as brown and cracked as a walnut, to explain the rules of the debate.

"Everyone knows by now that some people, both on Akron and on the space station, think that something's going to happen. The difference between this debate and an election is that no-one wins, no-one loses. If you want to stay you stay; and if you want to leave, you leave. One side want to leave. They're the *Refu-gees*, and they get six minutes. The other side wants to stay. They're the *Refu-zees*, and they also get six minutes. At the end of it you out there decide your verdict, your decision, your choice. You stay or you go, and no-one forces you to do either." He leaned forward to the camera and winked one blue eye. "But you must do one or the other."

"Tonight," he continued, "each side has its say. They drew lots before we went on air, and first word goes to the Refu-zees." As his face was replaced on screen by that of her father, Laurel drew breath. She'd half expected it. He was widely respected across Akron as a scholar and a distinguished citizen, so it made sense for the Refu-zees to use him as a spokesman. If anyone could make blind prejudice look respectable, it was him. He smiled, slightly nervously, and began his message.

"We have built up this planet. Many of us have devoted our lives to it. Here is everything we own, everything we've done." It was a straightforward emotional appeal, but Laurel winced at the amateurish production. Her father's speech was well written, but he simply delivered it straight to camera with no variation. Whoever had made this was relying on the message itself, rather than using any of the techniques which would have reinforced it. She thought of the video they had put together, and how she could have improved her father's own speech. As he spoke of the wonder of their planet, she would have shown dawn breaking over the green mountain mists of Kandaloo; Auriga slipping down to rest over the sands of the Golden Desert; the night sky, ablaze with the splendour of a globular cluster. The content, too, was amateurish. The Refu-zees were appealing to a sentimental sense of home, stressing the beauty of the planet and the strength of the community. This would not stand up against her own presentation. What use was a strong community and a place to call home when it was torn apart in cosmic explosion?

As his speech came to an end, even she was surprised to find she had been daydreaming through the second half of it; six minutes was too long to address the camera straight without any variation. She knew at that minute that her own appeal was going to blow her father's out of the water.

Dr Lindberg came on first, serious and concerned.

"There is bad news for Akron," he told his audience bluntly. "We cannot prevent it, but we might escape it." The camera cut to the scientist in Deep Lab, the water tank flashing and pinging behind him as he spoke.

"The normal neutrino count causes about one collision a week," Joseph explained. "Look at it now." He pointed, and the camera closed in on the frantic activity in the tank.

The picture changed to Blake in the Space Station.

"This type of change has been recorded three times before," he explained, pointing to lines which moved along charts as he spoke. "On Theta Orionid, on Delta Crux and on Himmelberg. In each case the star went nova. In each case its planets were destroyed."

Laurel sat forwards in her seat, full of anticipation as her section started. With Blake's help on the scientific details she had programmed a simple graphic to illustrate the nova process. Most people on Akron had never even left the planet and had little concept of the scale of Akron, never mind the universe. They could not understand the level of devastation the nova would cause, and without this visualisation they could never sufficiently fear it. By producing a graphic simulation she had hoped to persuade people of the seriousness of the event.

The graphic began with the familiar brown and white sphere of Akron, filling the screen. Laurel had wanted to put the planet at the heart of the story, to really bring home what the nova would do to the viewers. It hung in the sky, Auriga slowly appearing over its eastern edge, its glare filling the screen. Laurel had used Van to narrate the voice-over because his voice had a rich and compelling timbre to it.

"When a star goes nova," Van's voice came in, "it expands suddenly." As he spoke, the circumference of Auriga suddenly burst outward. "Its temperature rises by hundreds of degrees, then by thousands." The expanding image of the star grew brighter. Any reddish tint was swallowed up first by bright yellow, then brilliant white. Flares rose from its surface.

"Some of the outer layers are stripped away," Van's voice continued, as some of the prominences on the simulation were violently propelled outwards into space. "The inner planets are vaporized," he went on, and the simulation cut briefly to show the tiny planet *Zephyr*, closest to the star, as it was atomized by the explosive wave. Laurel caught her breath as beautiful Akron came on screen again, and Van's voice continued remorselessly.

"When the first radiation wave reaches Akron, all life will be destroyed instantly. The plasma stream will strip away the atmosphere." In the simulation, the blast reached Akron and animal and plant life were shown to expire. Again to personalise the story, Laurel had made a feature of a family of parroderms, a species of friendly, furry, tree-dwelling animals which everyone liked. She showed them choking to death in the blast, their bodies burning up in the heat, and finally their bones crumbled to powder and blown away in the heat storm which swept the planet. It took seconds. Van was still talking.

"After the atmosphere is gone the temperature will rise so high that sulphur and lead from inside the planet will become liquid and flow up to the surface."

For this Laurel had conjured up an image reminiscent of hell. Blue-burning sulphur flows erupted across the surface, and lakes of liquid metal steamed and shone under a dark sky. It was a nightmare.

"Finally," intoned Van, "what remains of Akron is lifeless forever, a dead planet circling a dead star." There was a brief clip of a murderous red world silently orbiting the feeble remains of a star. The presentation, carefully timed to six minutes, allowed for a moment's silence as the audience took in true meaning of a nova.

Dr Lindberg appeared with the final message. "This is what the nova will do, but fortunately we have seen it coming. Our calls for help have been answered and hundreds of ships are heading here now to take you to safety. There is room for all of us to evacuate, but we must do so now. I wish you all a safe journey and a safe arrival."

The screen went blank. Laurel leaned back thoughtfully. The question was: would it work?

8. Evacuation

Laurel was awoken in the middle of the night by a dull throbbing roar in the darkness outside. She struggled out of bed and saw them immediately through the window. Ships. Hundreds of ships, one after another ascending on pillars of flame from the spaceport. She stood there enthralled, watching them climb into the night in an endless procession. She knew immediately how the vote must have gone. The evacuation was in full swing, and did not stop for something as trivial as night.

Her suspicions were confirmed the next morning. Blake called to deliver the verdict: of those who voted, roughly ninety percent voted with the *Refu-gees* for immediate evacuation.

"And of course," he explained cheerfully, "since the first phases of evacuation were already complete, many of those now voting to leave had previously elected to stay." Blake estimated that only a few hundred people still held out as *Refu-zees*, although Laurel had to assume this would include her own parents.

Laurel was fully aware that breakfast would not be a comfortable event that morning. As she walked down the corridor to the dining room she thought about how her father had been made to look like a fool during the broadcast the night before. He probably blamed at least part of that broadcast on his daughter. On top of this, he really did believe he was right,

85

and she felt pained to see him so roundly defeated, even if she did not believe in what he stood for. She found him sitting at the table, hunched over his coffee. He had clearly spent the night vainly trying to rally support as the population deserted the *Refu-zees* by the thousand. However, her initial trepidation was dispelled by the warmth with which he greeted his daughter. After an exchange of greetings, she sat down to eat.

"When are you leaving?" he enquired.

"Maybe tomorrow, maybe the day after. It depends what gets done. What are your plans?" This was her delicate way of asking whether he had decided to evacuate with the others. Her father looked resigned.

"We're leaving tomorrow," he told her, finally. "There's no reason to stay any more, even if nothing happens. The Akron we know is already destroyed. The station has robbed Akron of its people, and with them go our communities and culture. And they robbed us of our livelihood, of course. There is no reason to stay without the Torquada."

Laurel dropped her spoon back onto the table. "What of the Torquada?"

Her father merely sighed, and slumped further on to the table. "I have worked on the Torquada's site my entire life. It was my life's work. I used to play at its feet as a boy and assumed, one day, I would visit the site in old age. Now it is gone there is nothing left for me on Akron."

"Gone!" Laurel was astonished. "Who took it?"

"Your lot were behind it, I assume. Tremayne came to collect it last night, after the broadcast. He had a document naming him the legal guardian and protector of the Torquada during the evacuation." He smiled sadly. "Perhaps it is for the best," he continued. "At least it will not be on Akron if the storm comes."

"But it belongs to everyone," Laurel exclaimed angrily. No matter what they did, Tremayne still had enough money and influence to persuade crooked lawyers and judges to support his cause. "And what of the curator?"

"He will stay." Her father said, sombrely. "Tremayne offered to take him, but he wanted to stay on Akron, where he found harmony." He looked sad. "I wish I could too."

After breakfast, Laurel left for the spaceport on her scooter. Her neighbourhood was virtually deserted, and she didn't see another soul until she hit the main route to the port. She shuddered during her journey, looking at the empty streets. The houses did not look as though they had been abandoned in a hurry: children's toys did not lie upturned in gardens, doors were not left open. Laurel had seen her neighbours tidying their houses before they left, cleaning and stacking crockery, taking out their rubbish, setting everything in order. They even locked their doors as they stepped out into the sun one last time. The sun that would, within a few days or less, engulf those same doors in flame and vaporize the houses completely. She chuckled uneasily at the strangeness of it, but was grateful they had chosen to leave in dignity, not panicked flight.

At the spaceport, Laurel was stunned by the vivid contrast between the scene before her and chaos she had met upon her landing. What had been random and disorganized motion was now smooth and efficient. Stewards met those who arrived and directed them to the appropriate areas. Guidance videos explained the process as new refugees arrived, and loudspeakers summoned them when it was time to leave. Everyone took the luck of the draw. A family might enjoy their passage out aboard a sleek space yacht, or they might be placed in the cargo hold of utility freighter. Whilst the children boasted or grumbled about the quality of their ride, the parents were glad to be getting one at all.

Laurel stood for a while in the observation lounge to watch the succession of departing ships. They touched down, refuelled, loaded up with passengers, and took off again. She followed a small courier ship from landing to take-off. As it landed in clouds of steam she watched pipes being connected and trucks pull alongside. Then came the passengers, boarding quickly except for one elderly lady who had to be helped up the ramp. Laurel counted twenty-three of them. The ship would normally take about seven or eight, but someone, probably on her own station, had precisely calculated the maximum weight which could be lifted to escape velocity. She watched the hatch hum into place and close with a satisfying *clunk*. There was a short wait, then the jets of flame flickered and the spaceport reverberated to the roar of the engines as it lifted its way into the sky. The whole process took less than thirty minutes.

She glanced at Auriga anxiously, but the star looked deceptively benign. What had Blake said? They now had two days, perhaps less. She shivered. They had done rather well, Laurel supposed. The bulk of the evacuation was over, and at the rate they were moving ships and people off the planet, it would soon be down to picking up the stragglers and late-comers, and those among the *Refu-zees* who changed their mind at the last minute.

There was nothing she could do about the evacuation, it would run its course. So that left only the Torquda. On an impulse she called the *Lodestar*.

"Ah, the girl from the temple." Tremayne called out. "We meet again, although in better circumstances." He toasted her with a glass of champagne, which he drained dramatically before turning back to her. "I found out a great deal about you, Laurel. I enjoyed the show you helped to put together last night. It was quite a performance."

Laurel was in no mood to tolerate one of Tremayne's speeches. "Where is the Torquada?" she demanded angrily.

"She's quite safe, my dear, and looking forward to her voyage. I have the architects working on a new home now. No dusty, desert cave for this beauty. Only the best."

"How did you do this? It belongs to Akron!"

"Well, I owe you all on the space station a favour. Your nova star put that priceless relic in danger, and as in a moment of

88

8. EVACUATION

philanthropic charity I of course volunteered to protect it. I am now her legal guardian, and there is nothing you or that curious friend of yours can do about it."

Laurel was furious, but knew she was defeated. Tremayne continued.

"And if you see your young friend again do tell him that I will remember him." There was no mistaking the threat in his voice.

"And I'm sure he'll remember you," Laurel said. "And your shoes."

Pure hate flashed across Tremayne's face. "Fine. This has been a charming conversation, but I must make haste. Torquadas do not fly themselves to safety. I regret of course that I cannot now take any evacuees with me. They no longer fit in with my plans."

Laurel was appalled. "People are depending on you!"

"Yes," Tremayne smirked, "but no-one I'm likely to meet again in a hurry."

He severed the connection, leaving Laurel staring at the empty screen, still fuming at his arrogance and the corrupt legal system that let him run rings around the law. Depressingly, Laurel had to assume he would get away with it.

She felt a movement behind her, and span round to find Van had come up behind her, and had followed her conversation with Tremayne.

"I thought I'd find you here," he said. "I didn't expect to find *him* being so smug, though."

Laurel sighed. "I don't know what to do about the Torquada."

"Simple. We get it back."

"But he's the legal guardian, if we try to take it we'll be stealing. He might be able to hire corrupt judges to grant him ownership, but we can't hire them to let us off for theft." Van's amber eyes clouded for a few moments as Laurel watched him thinking it through.

"It will now be the most closely guarded object on the planet. They are not good odds: one ship, Tremayne and his thugs against the two of us. We could attack him in space, ship to ship. I've no idea what my ship can do, but I'll bet it can outshoot and outrun a ship designed for champagne cruises rather than fighting. But I guess there's no estimating how many people might get killed. Including us," he added with a quick grin.

"If we can't take it by force, what solution can there be?"

"Well," said Van, coming to a conclusion. "He has to give it back to us voluntarily."

"Why should he do that?" asked Laurel incredulously.

"Because we will have something he wants more than the Torquada," Van replied with a glint in his eye that suggested mischief.

* * * * *

Laurel felt guilty. This was probably her last ever evening on Akron; it would be her last memory of the world which had given her birth and nurtured her youth. She should really have spent it with her parents, making up their differences and talking about their times together. But Laurel knew it would have been strained, and she chose instead to spend Akron's last evening with Van, showing him one of her favourite places on the planet. Her parents would probably spend their last evening talking by the fire as always. In the morning they would be evacuated on the *Arcturus*.

Laurel had brought Van to the Trembling Lake. They took a brief swim to cool down, for a moment forgetting the danger that hung over them and simply enjoying playing in the waters. As Auriga began to set on the horizon, they lit a fire on the shore and lay down on the beach to dry out.

8. EVACUATION

"Why is it called the Trembling Lake?" Van asked, shivering slightly in the cold and drawing nearer to the fire.

"Wait," Laurel whispered as Auriga vanished behind the mountains and the sky gradually dimmed. Laurel stared out upon the lake, waiting for it to happen.

When it happened she nudged Van and pointed. He followed the direction. Tiny lights were shimmering on the surface of the water, almost dancing, and the water itself throbbed and trembled too. It was pure magic, just as she had seen it so often as a child. Van was enthralled.

"Why is it dancing?" he asked softly, as if afraid that a loud noise might alarm whatever it was. Laurel laughed.

"You won't startle it," she said. "It's caused by millions of tiny organisms which rise to the surface in the evenings. They release a gas which ignites in the air. My parents used to bring me here as a child."

"It's very pretty," Van remarked.

Laurel looked at his back, glistening in the firelight, and saw rough dull white scars scattered here and there across it. She wondered what Van had been through to mark him like that.

"You don't talk about yourself much, do you Van?" she commented.

"Not very much to talk about: I don't remember anything," Van replied sadly. "I liked it when you did all the talking, when you were teaching me stuff for the first few days."

"I liked that, too," she remarked, smiling.

Van flicked a pebble into the lake, where it hit with a satisfying *plunk*.

"You know, I can't help thinking I'm going to forget all this." He swept his hand around. "Everything I've seen and experienced, Everything I've learned. Everyone I've known. When this is over, whatever it is, and however it ends, I think that ship will take me away, and that I will sleep again. When I wake up my memories of this will be gone." He paused. "It may have happened many times before. And all this will have been for nothing."

He fell silent. Laurel reflected on his situation. If everything he had learned, everything he had seen, was simply wiped from his memory then the boy who woke up would no longer be Van. He would have none of Van's memories, or his loves, hopes and fears. Laurel shivered as she suddenly thought that others might have thought this about him before, and been right about it. Who were these people he had once known, but could never remember?

"So you see, it's difficult to talk," Van said. Laurel thought how lost he looked. She reached over and held his hand.

They sat in silence, staring at the lake trembling before them. Eventually the dancing ceased and the lake became still again, reflecting in its calm waters the lights of the distant ships, still climbing one after another into the heavens. Laurel again remembered why she was here on Akron, and sighed upon realisation that the peacefulness of the evening must come to an end.

They packed away their picnic carefully, and stamped on the last remains of the fire. She smiled to herself when she realised she was behaving like all the others. Would it really matter if there was a wildfire tonight, given the fire that was going to come within days from the sky?

Before they left Van held out a package, smiling. "A present, to thank you for a lovely evening." Laurel was surprised, and unwrapped the package slowly. It was something she had never seen before, a curious mass of wire and silicon. She looked up at Van, puzzled.

"It's a communications artery governor," he explained. "See, here's the central barium crystal."

"Um, just what I always wanted!" she exclaimed jokingly. "What does it do?"

8. EVACUATION

"Don't ask what it does, ask what a ship can't do without it," Van said. "The answer is nothing. Certainly not fly."

It dawned on Laurel in a flash. "You took this from the *Lodestar*," she cried accusingly. Van smiled back sheepishly.

"Was it dangerous?" she demanded.

"Very." Van's eyes danced.

"What do I do with it?" she asked.

"You wait. Tremayne will call. First he'll bully. Then he'll threaten. And then he'll trade. At that point you can swap what he has and wants for what he hasn't and needs."

"Simple as that," breathed Laurel, delighted.

9. Panic

Van was wrong on two counts, but right on the one that mattered. Tremayne did not bully, and he did not threaten. He had left three messages on Laurel's communicator by the time she woke up, still basking in the pleasure of a well-spent evening. It would be the last night she ever had on Akron, and was more memorable and pleasurable than most.

When she finally called Tremayne he had none of the bored, sarcastic manner which he normally employed to show people how unimportant they were. He looked crisp and serious and came straight to the point.

"Good of you to return my calls," he began. "You have something which belongs to me, I believe." There was no accusation there, just a statement of fact.

"You have something which does *not* belong to you, I believe?" she responded. Tremayne gave a weak smile with no humour in it.

"Must we still talk about that? Someone took the Communications Artery Governor from my ship, and whoever it was took a lot of trouble to get it. They learned the layout of my ship, they eluded my guards, and they evaded an extremely sophisticated alarm system. I have no evidence, but if I had to bet I'd say it was that rather strange young man you hang around with."

Laurel nodded patiently to herself. She held all the cards, and could afford to play with Tremayne a little. Finally she broke her silence. "Sorry, did you have a point?"

"Yes," Tremayne retorted angrily. "Obviously. I need that CAG to get off this filthy rock of a planet, and if your scientists are correct I'm going to need it sooner rather than later."

Laurel nodded solemnly. "That is indeed a problem, yes."

Tremayne leaned forward towards the screen, as though confiding in her. "I know that you must have it. You must return it to me immediately."

"Why should I do that?" asked Laurel innocently.

"If you don't, we'll still be on this planet when the star explodes. My crew and I will all die. You would be saving our lives."

Laurel scoffed. "How rich for a man with no better nature to try to appeal to mine. I will not let you take the Torquada."

"Ah, a straight swap? My statue for the CAG?" Tremayne stared into the screen. "Well, sorry. No deal. I intend to keep the Torquada. I've worked too hard for it and I'm not giving it up now. Instead I propose a better deal, something that certainly *should* appeal to your better nature."

Laurel rolled her eyes. Tremayne was being absurd if he expected her to believe he was prepared to die rather than surrender the stolen relic. What else could he offer? Money was all he had. She waited without anticipation for his proposal. It surprised her.

"I'm sure you are aware Auriga may already be in its last day. You need as much help as you can get. If you return the CAG, and I mean return it *now*, I will take as many of your evacuees as my ship will hold. That's the bargain. If you say yes, you save their lives. If you say no, my crew and I die along with your evacuees, and all because of a silly missing component"

9. PANIC

He was adamant. He made it look as though this were his final offer.

"You promised that once already and broke it when it suited you," she accused.

"Yes, my dear, but that was a promise. This is a bargain. I might break promises when it suits me, but I never break a bargain. When you do that no-one will ever deal with you again."

Laurel hesitated. When it came down to it, the Torquada was worth rather less than a shipment of lives. What was saving an inert piece of sculpture compared to saving lives, restoring families, maintaining friendships? She remembered what Tremayne had said, about needing to know when your opponent held the cards. She had no idea whether he was bluffing or whether he was really prepared to die rather than give up the Torquada. She decided she couldn't afford to call his bluff.

"Okay, then," she conceded. "I return the CAG to you, and you agree to take as many evacuees as your ship can carry? Correct?" Tremayne nodded in confirmation.

"And there's one other thing I want," Laurel told him.

Tremayne's face became intent. His eyes narrowed slightly. "The bargain seems quite sufficient as it is."

"Maybe you have ideas about taking revenge on Van some time in the future and levelling the score. I want you to lay off. You're to leave him alone and let it rest."

Tremayne looked thoughtful. He stroked his bushy grey eyebrows, and finally smiled. "Done," he announced. "Though you don't know what that costs me. All right. I promise to leave Van alone."

"I don't want a promise," remarked Laurel. "This is part of the deal."

"Part of the deal," confirmed Tremayne, laughing now. He could afford to; he'd won.

Laurel set the transaction in motion immediately, arranging for the spaceport authorities to pick out the suitable evacuees. When they had all boarded the transport, she handed the CAG to a retired space officer who seemed to be making the trip by himself.

"This is important, look after it," she told the trim white-haired figure as she handed it to him. The retired officer snapped to attention.

"As though my life depends on it."

"Good," Laurel said. "It does."

The planet was emptying out. Her parents had checked aboard the *Arcturus*, and Van was in orbit helping the space station to direct the late ships into suitable trajectories. There were so many ships waiting for their window to launch into quantum space that they were at grave risk of bumping into each other – or "tearing into each other," as Van put it. Collisions could be messy at such speeds.

Meanwhile, Laurel had to help her colleagues deal with the few hundred stragglers still on Akron. Although there were now so few, they took a great deal of time and energy to deal with. By mid morning Laurel felt drained. She stopped for a glass of chilled juice and watched the chaos in the spaceport. Huge piles of possessions lay dropped in the hallways, accumulated and abandoned over the days by distressed families and rummaged through by scavengers seeking anything they might be able to smuggle aboard with them.

Among the heat and the chaos, worse news was yet to come. Her communicator beeped. It was Blake.

"Hi Blake," she said, pleased to see him. He was not in a cheerful mood.

9. PANIC

"Go look at Auriga," he told her curtly. She dropped her juice and dashed to a window at once. She'd been so busy helping to get people organized on to their assigned transports that she hadn't had time for any casual sight-seeing.

She saw it at once. Auriga had changed. The star was noticeably larger, and its colour had become more intense. There was barely a hint of orange now, just a clear bright whiteness.

"We think it could blow at any time," came Blake's urgent voice. "Everyone has to get out now, including you," he added. "I mean *now*."

As though to reinforce the urgency of his message the spaceport loudspeakers started barking instructions. All evacuees were to report to their assigned ships immediately. Those with no ship assigned would be given one at the gates.

"Laurel?" Blake called. "Laurel, you have to take off immediately. Can you do that?" Laurel thought quickly. Were her parents safely on board their ship? Could the transport make it to the Lodestar? Could all the remaining ships get away in time?

She looked at the crowds. The emergency announcement had startled them, and once they got outside they could see the changes in Auriga. A sense of panic was beginning to rise at the spaceport as word spread and those with no assigned escape route fought over the few spaces they could find.

"I mean *now*," Blake shouted. Laurel reached her decision. Events could take care of themselves. Now, just for once, she had to take care of Laurel.

"Now it is," she told him. "I'll take one of the shuttles."

There was a shuttle park outside the spaceport which wasn't being used in the evacuation. The shuttles took just one passenger, and most of the evacuees had never been in a spaceship before, never mind knew how to fly a shuttle. Of course she didn't really know how to fly a real shuttle either,

99

Laurel reflected, apart from what she head learned in the simulator. Whilst taking off was easy, spinning out of control back into the planet was most likely easier.

As she gunned her scooter towards the shuttles, she saw a crowd storming toward the perimeter of the spaceport. She pulled up briefly to watch them, and recognized a few faces. These were some of the diehard *Refu-zees*. Now they were converging on the spaceport, and many of them seemed to be armed. Those that had refused a flight out in good time seemed determined to take one now, even if they had to take it from someone else. A few of them shouted as they saw her uniform, but Laurel sped off towards the shuttle park. She wanted to be well on her way before things turned ugly.

She heard an explosion from the terminal building as she pulled up next to a shuttle. She leaped off her scooter and looked back. People were streaming out the terminal towards the runways. The building itself was giving off thick black smoke, and was swallowed up in flames before her eyes. She hurried up the ramp, stumbling over the access code for the shuttle. She heard the distinct crack of a molecular disrupter. The crowd was using firearms. She opened the hatch and climbed aboard.

The orderly and dignified evacuation had descended into a ragged tail-end of confusion. Ships were taking off from every part of the huge complex. She watched their trails as they made their last-minute escape, Laurel uttered a silent wish that they would make it. On the ground was more confusion. Figures swarmed over the remaining ships as people fought to gain a last place on them. She heard the crack of firearms between the roar of ships' engines, and saw figures fall prostrate to the ground. Smoke was rising from every part of the complex, with the main terminal building now engulfed in flames.

Laurel shuddered and sealed the hatch. She would be well out of it. She settled into her chair and turned on the com-link so she could listen in on the chatter of the departing ships.

9. PANIC

"This is Arcturus, *does anybody read?"* called a voice over the link. Laurel listened intently. That was the ship her parents were on. Would they escape in time?

"This is Arcturus, *unable to complete take-off. Does anybody read?"* Laurel's heart sank. They had not managed to take off. The voice was young, perhaps that of a newly-qualified officer. He sounded uncertain.

Laurel reached for the com-switch, but a voice boomed in before she could press it.

"This is Antares, Arcturus. *What seems to be the problem?"* It was an older voice, calm and authoritative.

"Antares, thank the stars for that! This is Arcturus. *The Refu-zees have stormed the cargo hold. We were carrying the maximum already. We're too heavy. If we take off now we won't reach escape velocity. What do we do?"* The young officer sounded desperate.

"Steady now, Arcturus." The older man was reassuring. *"How many of them do you estimate?"*

"I don't know. Maybe a couple of dozen."

"Are they into the ship itself?"

"Negative, Antares. *The airlocks are all sealed. Just in the cargo bay,"* replied the young officer.

The older voice drawled. *"Okay, Arcturus. You can't achieve escape velocity, but you can get a low orbit. Head for orbit and then flush the cargo bay. Then do a second burn for escape velocity. Understood?"*

There was a long pause. *"You mean, jettison the boarders into space? Kill them?"*

"It's standard procedure," the older man told him. *"It's the only way to save your passengers."*

The young officer from the *Arcturus* finally came on. *"Understood,"* he replied. His voice wavered slightly. *"Thanks for your help, Antares."*

The connection was severed. Laurel watched the big freighter rise up into the sky on jets of flame, before the main engines ignited and the ship soared aloft. She watched as her mother and father were taken away from the only planet they had known. She thought of the Refu-zees, so desperate to escape the planet that they had boarded a ship that could not carry them. They would have felt the take-off and think they were safely away from the planet. Yet in a few moments there would be the hiss of air as the cargo door cranked open, and terror would take over. Laurel shuddered. It was time for her to leave as well.

She strapped herself in and went through the take-off preparation sequence. She had done this a hundred times in the simulator up on the space station, and going through it now was somehow calming. The repetition helped to focus her mind, and forget the riots going on outside: Fuel, check. Power, check. Trajectory, check. Controls, check.

She was about to launch when Blake came through on her com-link.

"Laurel?" There was something odd about his voice

"What is it, Blake?" His face appeared on screen. "I'm just about through the take-off sequence. Can it wait?"

"I suppose it can. Don't head for the station, though." Laurel frowned to herself. This was strange.

"Why not? Where else am I supposed to go?" Her shuttle was only suitable for short journeys. It could not go into quantum space, and could never outrun the nova explosion.

"We've finished co-ordinating the evacuation as best we can and put the station under way on full power. We're now going to try to outrun the blast wave. If you come looking for us, we'll be gone."

Laurel nodded slowly. The plan had always been to evacuate the planet and then move the station out. It was just as vulnerable as Akron itself. Unless the station was out of the way the radiation storm would reach it a few seconds after the planet was incinerated.

"We're not even sure we'll be fast enough. It might happen too soon." Blake explained. "There's a lot of mass here to accelerate, and it's going to take us time to get up to a decent speed. If the star blows before then the blast wave will beat us to it."

"What do you suggest I do?" she asked.

"Just go at maximum velocity away from Auriga. Get as far away as fast as possible and... well, hope for the best." Laurel swallowed heavily. What if her best wasn't good enough?

"It really has been great working with you, Laurel," Blake said sadly. With a shock Laurel realized he was saying goodbye. In his clumsy, decidedly unsentimental way he was signing off.

"I'm sure we'll make it, Blake. I'll see you all on the other side of all this." But even as she said it, Laurel regretted the words 'you all'. She cared about the rest of the space station, of course, but she cared about him most. Any thoughts about how she might express her appreciation for that friendship were dispelled by a sharp crack on the hull of the shuttle. The whole thing rocked around her.

"What was that?" asked a worried Blake.

She reached over to activate the external view screens. People were everywhere, swarming round the base of the shuttle, climbing up the engine tubes, and banging on the side of the shuttle with what looked like a metal bar. Their faces seemed completely demented, consumed by rage. These were some of the people who had broken into the spaceport, the ones who had spread fire and destruction through its facilities. She remembered the young officer on the *Arcturus*, "They stormed the ship and entered the cargo hold."

The shuttle shuddered as another crack sounded on the hull. They could do serious damage to the shuttle. It wasn't designed for even elementary combat. She couldn't take off with them there, either. The blast from the engines would vaporise them.

"Problems, Blake. Hold on," she said tersely. She switched to external intercom.

"What do you want?" she demanded. "You are endangering yourselves and the safety of this shuttle."

A man's face thrust in front of one of the cameras. Blood streaked his face and matted his hair. He shouted his reply so loudly that Laurel flinched from the force of it.

"We want to get out," he screamed. "Take us with you."

"That is impossible," she told them over the intercom. "These shuttles are built for just one passenger. There isn't room or fuel for more."

The blood-caked man was adamant. "We'll take our chances on that," he screamed. Laurel was aghast.

The communicator bleeped. It was Blake.

"Laurel, you have to lift off now. You cannot waste another second. The star is going to blow and you probably don't have enough time as it is." He looked desperate.

Laurel *was* desperate. The banging intensified, and from the outside camera she could see more of them climbing up towards the cockpit. If they reached the window, they could probably break it open.

"I can't take off while they're on the ship," she told Blake.

"Laurel, it's you or them. They had their chance. Don't let them take yours," cried Blake. But Laurel knew she couldn't do it. She couldn't press a switch and send a dozen people into an incandescent oblivion. This was it.

She saw a shadow across the cockpit. One of the assailants had reached it. He stared in, wild eyes darting about. Laurel froze in terror. She knew the man, he had been a friend of her father. She had gone to school with his daughter, eaten supper with them more times than she could remember. Now he stood crouched before her, desperate and wild, wielding a metal bar torn from one of the chairs in the departure lounge. Either she started the engines, killed him and escaped, or they died together. But still, she could not make that decision.

The screen in front of her flickered and Blake's face disappeared. In his place was Van. He stared levelly at her, his face completely serious. He made no attempt to argue.

"Laurel, I order you to hit the take-off button immediately. Now." The last word was shouted with great force. Laurel reached forward and hit the ignition switch without pausing for thought. She felt that the decision had been taken for her. What she couldn't do when Blake asked her, she did when Van commanded her.

The engines started with a mighty roar. Her father's friend was forcibly torn from view as flames and steam billowed up around the ship. The shuttle soared aloft and surged into the sky, leaving burnt wreckage and human debris in its wake.

10. Flight

Tremayne regretted his generosity the moment the transport arrived and the pathetic band of riffraff descended from its hatch. He had felt claustrophobic on those few occasions his yacht was host to ambassadors and royalty, but now it was to be a refugee camp for a dozen squalid families. He shuddered. He had always arranged his life so that he was spared the everyday contact with the underclass; now he would have to endure it for days.

He silently cursed his occasional propensity for telling the truth. Why did he have to tell the girl the *Lodestar* could take so many passengers? He could as easily have claimed just a handful and she'd still have given him the CAG. Still, they could be avoided.

He summoned the mate.

"I want it understood that I am to be left alone in my private suite and not disturbed by our passengers under any circumstances. Is that clear?"

The mate, an amply built middle-aged figure, coughed apologetically. He had served ten years with Tremayne and knew his moods well.

"Sorry, sir. Your private suite will be accommodating some of our guests," he informed his boss. "You asked us to take the maximum; that means all the available space."

Tremayne sank into an even blacker mood. He looked out at the wretched band trailing towards his beautiful yacht, carrying the minimum of possessions. They really were hopeless, but it was too late to turn them back now. He glared at the mate.

"Install the CAG and get them stowed as quickly as possible," he ordered. "If we must tolerate this, let's at least make it swift." He stared again at the swollen image of Auriga. "We may not have much time left as it is. I take it the Torquada is stowed?"

"Indeed, sir, the only cargo we've retained. There's no weight to spare, once the people are on board."

"Well, one must do what can one for our heritage?" Tremayne said.

It took just twenty minutes to get everyone stowed on board. Some had bunks, but since his elegant chairs had been unloaded to make room for more people, the unfortunate majority were assigned a piece of floor and a blanket. Tremayne shuddered again. He would have to have the ship fumigated afterwards to remove the smell of sweat, the stench of people.

Tremayne stepped out of the hatch for a last breath of fresh air. His last look at the bleak world, a dreadful planet whose only achievement in a million years was to produce the Torquada. He looked up again at the star. It might have been his imagination, but it seemed to have grown bigger and brighter than when he last saw it. The edges seemed almost to throb. He shook the thought from his head. Time to go.

He walked back up the ramp and closed the hatch. Just before the door sealed and pressurised, he thought he caught sight of a small figure standing outside the ship. He activated the com-link.

"Did we leave anyone?" he asked the mate.

"No sir. All on board and stowed," came the reply.

10. FLIGHT

Tremayne peered through the window in the hatch. It was a small girl, standing uncertainly in front of the ship, dirty and dishevelled. Her clothes were torn, her fair hair bedraggled, a torn and insect-chewed stuffed toy parroderm hanging limply in one hand.

"There is some sort of girl outside the ship."

The mate checked his readings to confirm it. "She must be well away from the ship when the engines fire or she'll be fried," he added.

Tremayne sighed. For all his riches and influence, he still found himself doing the grunt work. He reopened the hatch and went down to the girl. She looked up with big eyes, her entire face smudged with dirt but for two channels cut by tears.

He tried to wave the girl away with a shooing motion, but either she didn't understand or was too upset to do anything about it. She stood staring at him expressionlessly.

"The star is about to explode," Tremayne explained loudly. "If you could just step back twenty feet?"

The girl smiled and ran towards him, throwing both arms around his legs, hugging his finest moleskin trousers. Tremayne recoiled and tried to push the girl away, but she only clung harder. They had to leave immediately.

"Can we take her?" he asked his first mate.

"Negative, chief. We're on absolute maximum weight. We'd have to ditch one of the others if we did."

Tremayne forcibly tore the girl off his legs. Her parents had probably been among the deranged *Refu-zees*, he reasoned. What duty did he owe to her if even her own parents had fought for her right to die in a giant cosmic firework? She stumbled from his force and fell on to the ground, where she sat in the dirt, hugging her little stuffed animal.

He was part way up the gangway when he felt something enter his mind. He paused, one hand on the railing. Whatever it was seemed real. It was clinical, dispassionate; part of himself, and it was questioning him. Was it a conscience? Tremayne snorted inwardly at the thought. He got this far without the need for one, and he certainly did not need a conscience now. No, he sensed the feeling was not of regret or remorse: it was more subtle than that. It was questioning his sense of the fitness of things.

It was a part of himself that was gently searching through his mind. Tremayne felt it move through him like a cool wind. It reminded him of the sea-mists which sometimes washed against his ocean-side home on Tarantos III. They would come like a wall of mist out of the sea, probing with ghostly grey fingers at the doors and windows, searching for openings. It was as though those ghostly fingers were probing through his mind. Was his sense of priorities appropriate? Did the things he rated as important actually count for much? Wealth and power were fine, he enjoyed them and felt no regret at all about his pursuit of them, but did he use them aptly?

These were delicate, challenging questions which aimed at the heart of his scale of values. But what was it about himself they were searching for?

Suddenly Tremayne knew what it was. He remained motionless on the gangway as the realization flowed through him like electricity. It was harmony! Great nebulae! The ugly old bat with the crumpled wings had delivered the goods after all. The old man had been wrong when he said there was no room in his life for harmony. Here it was, washing over his mind with full force. Here it was, telling him to balance the forces and drives in his life, telling him to allow more weight to the things which counted.

He turned and looked down at the child, still sobbing on the ground at the foot of the gangway. He heard the anxious voice of the mate calling from the hatch above.

"Sir, we must leave."

10. FLIGHT

"We take the child," Tremayne called out, turning back down the gangway.

"We can't. We're too heavy," the mate told him.

Tremaybe paused. Could he do it? A sense of the fitness of things.

"Unload the Torquada," he ordered. "We take the girl instead."

"Chief?" The mate was thunderstruck.

"You heard. Unload it. We take the girl." As he reached the bottom, he swept the girl into his arms and carried her up the steps.

"Yes, chief, doing it now." After ten years the mate knew when and how to obey an order.

Tremayne stood with his arm on the little girl's shoulder as the relic was unloaded. He watched his men carry it down to the runway and carefully set it upright, at some distance from the *Lodestar*. So it was done.

They strapped in and completed the take-off procedure. As the *Lodestar* lifted off on its pencil of fire, Tremayne caught a final glimpse below him of the solitary, motionless figure left behind, casting its strange shadow on the runway. The ship disappeared into the skies, and the enigmatic shape was alone. Those ancient eyes, grown old in watching the days of a million years, now stared out impassively on the last day they would ever see.

* * * * *

Laurel stared at the fuel gauge in disbelief. She tapped it, but it refused to show a better reading.

"Are you there, Van?" she asked. His image flicked back on to the screen.

"Yes, I'm here." He looked at something off screen. "You're too slow. What happened?"

"The Refu-zees attacked the shuttle, I think my fuel line was damaged. I'm on an automatic escape trajectory, but the shuttle isn't fast enough. I'm not going to make escape velocity." Without more fuel or engine power she would plunge back to the planet, burning up in Akron's atmosphere long before reaching the surface.

"There's no way I'm going to make it." She tried increasing power to the main engines, which immediately cut out. She was coasting on a gentle trajectory that would never escape the pull of Akron's gravity.

"Your main engines have cut," said Van. "Do you still have positioning thrusters?" Yes, she did. She could move the position of the shuttle, but that was all. She tested them briefly to make sure.

"Yes, but that won't increase my forward velocity."

Van's voice was completely calm. "You don't need to," he told her. "I'm going to position my ship in front of you. All you have to do is dock with it."

"All?" Laurel laughed with anxiety. Hundreds of miles above a dying planet, on a collision course with an atmosphere that would shortly be stripped from the planet in a nova explosion. And all she had to do was align herself flawlessly into a strange ship.

"Van, I've never docked with anything before," she told him simply. He was incredulous.

"Don't they teach how to dock in the first week of training?" he queried. "It's a pretty essential manoeuvre."

"Well, give me a year or so," Laurel explained, her voice rising with the absurdness of the situation. "That's when I start my training. Until then, I know some dry facts about intergalactic protocol that might be of no use."

"Just imagine you're in the simulator. Same controls, same results. It's not a problem, really. Just be patient." He swallowed, and frowned. "You know, patient but quick. We don't have time to spare."

Laurel didn't reply. There was a simple difference between the simulator and real life. Foul up in a simulator and a red light flashed and you were out in time for an early tea. Foul it up in real life and you risked tearing open both ships and never having tea again.

A dark shadow came across the shuttle, and Laurel felt the temperature drop. She shivered. Van's ship was descending above her, manoeuvring itself into the correct position and matching her velocity. The ship still looked menacing and sinister, even after it had revealed some of its more pleasant secrets.

Laurel could see where Van had opened one of the rear docking bays. With relief she saw that it was designed to take much bigger ships, and she'd have plenty of room to manoeuvre.

Van was full of confident reassurance.

"Laurel, keep it slow, steady, and nothing sudden. Remember to under-play any movement, momentum does the rest."

Laurel felt her mouth go dry as she gave a short forward burst on the positioning thrusters. The tail of the shuttle reared up over the nose alarmingly as a forward spin started. Quickly she corrected with a counter burst. This was trickier than it seemed.

She decided to do it step by step. First she set her attitude so that she was lined up with Van's ship. She fixed the open docking bay against one of the bars on the cockpit window and kept it in the same position. She suppressed a small roll to starboard, and inched forward gradually towards the bay. Her burst had clearly been too aggressive, and the ship entered into a slight spin, taking the shuttle out of alignment. As she entered the bay, the shuttle's wing collided with the wall. It was clearly made from the same impenetrable substance as the outside of the ship, as the bay remained undamaged, whilst Laurel's wing was torn in half. The collision was violent, shaking Laurel in her chair. Her control panel flickered and died, the power gone.

"Are you all right? What's going on?" Van called out.

"I've lost a wing, power's out and I'm losing pressure," Laurel replied in panic. She stabbed at the control desk, hoping in vain for it to come back to life. She could feel the air inside the pod flushing into the vacuum outside. She was powerless in the shuttle, and the air wouldn't last long.

"You're in the bay at least. Hold on."

The bay doors closed shut and sealed the bay behind her in an instant. The room was repressurized, and the gravity field gradually brought up, so the shuttle gently floated to the ground.

"Docking successful, good job," Van told her. She looked down at her hands on the controls and saw the knuckles and fingertips were white with the intensity of her grip.

This was Laurel's first time on Van's ship, but she remembered Blake's initial scans, how she had spotted that there were no living quarters. The control room was cramped, and beyond it the small chamber with the sleeping pod in which Van had spent his voyage, and probably many previous ones.

"Did everyone else get away?" she asked, but Van shook his head.

"No. Most took off in time, but a few of the last ships were over-run by rioters. I don't think they'll make it now."

Laurel looked at Akron on the screen in the control room. Those people on her home planet were now doomed to be swallowed by the star under which they had lived for so long. And yet, even those who had managed to get off the planet still needed to get out of the system if they were to survive.

Van showed her a schematic of Auriga, around which radiated small red dots.

"Blake thinks it will blow in less than a day. These red dots mark the fleeing ships, heading at full speed out of the system.

10. FLIGHT

They have to get far enough from the star's distortion field to make the jump into quantum space."

Laurel stared at the schematic. Such a simple diagram, and yet it symbolised so much. On one of the red dots, the *Arcturus*, her parents would be sitting. She could imagine her mother in distress, her father comforting her but no less anxious. And in each ship, hundreds of such couples and families.

"Will they make it?" Laurel asked.

The amber eyes stared straight into hers. "I don't know," he said quietly. "I hope so."

"And what about us?" she wondered. Van smiled confidently.

"We'll make it. The moment you docked we went on to full power. If the blast holds off long enough we should be safe in quantum space by the time it comes."

"So what do we do in the meantime?"

Van switched the monitor back to the image of Auriga and looked at the clock. "We wait," he said.

And wait they did. Time passed slowly, and every minute felt like half an hour. Two hours into the wait, Van managed to patch a call through to the *Arcturus*. Laurel spoke to a young officer, quite possibly the one who had made the desperate decision to flush the boarders from the cargo hold. Laurel breathed an audible sigh of relief when he confirmed that her parents were safely on board. While she was not able to talk to them directly, the officer promised to pass on her love and wishes, and to let them know that she was safely aboard Van's ship.

'Safe' was a poor choice of word, however. As Laurel and Van waited to reach quantum space, they fretted about the unspoken thought that if the starburst came too soon, then they and the other ships would be consumed in its fire. Laurel found herself torn between a desire to get it over with and to end the suspense one way or the other, and the thought that the longer the wait went on, the more chance they would have of survival.

One relief which lightened their wait was a call from the *Lodestar*. It was made to the station, but Van intercepted the signal and put it up on screen so they could follow it.

"I repeat, this is *Lodestar*. Is there anyone with any kind of authority?"

Laurel was thrilled. There was no doubt it was Tremayne's voice. Sure enough the familiar features appeared on screen, though the picture kept breaking up.

"This is the Akron space station. How can I help?" It was Dr Lindberg, looking as calm and authoritative as ever.

"This is *Lodestar*. I would rather like to know, just for personal amusement you understand, when the star is going to blow." Laurel thought she detected something indefinably different about him.

Dr Lindberg looked thoughtful. He examined something off-screen.

"The neutrino count is at maximum. We expect the nova burst within twenty-four hours. Of course, you're rather more concerned about when in the next twenty-four hours." Tremayne nodded, expectantly. Lindberg stared straight into camera, knowing that ships throughout the system would be listening in. "I can't answer that, but if it happens within fifteen hours the blast wave will probably reach you before you are clear for a quantum jump. I'm afraid the odds are slightly worse for us. We'll need nearer to twenty hours, maybe more, before we are clear enough."

Tremayne looked lost in thought for a moment. "Thank you for that," he said. "It would be gratifying if our efforts paid off. We've been running with full power to main engines and all other systems shut down, including life support." As he said it he wiped the back of his hand over his forehead. Dr Lindberg raised his eyebrows.

10. FLIGHT

"You can't survive very long without life support," he told Tremayne.

"Nor in the blast wave of a nova star," was the curt reply. At that point the signal finally broke up. Laurel tuned to Van.

"Fifteen hours," she mused.

"Let's hope it's more," he replied.

It was less.

As the time dragged by, Laurel felt the need for sleep. At Van's suggestion she opted for a short nap. The only convenient place was the sleeping pod itself, in which Van had spent years in suspended animation. With the lid open it was less forbidding, and comfortable enough for Laurel to drift off into a troubled sleep. It was a sleep disturbed by scenes of rioting and burning, and of the panic-crazed faces of those who had left it too late. She kept seeing the image of the deranged face of her friend's father pressed against her cockpit as she hit the switch which swept him to oblivion. She felt herself shaking as the engines fired. No, she was being shaken.

She was being wakened by Van. From the look on his face she knew something was very wrong. Quickly she shook off the remaining effects of her brief nap and followed him into the control room. He pointed to the screen.

Quite obviously the star was at a critical point. It had greatly increased in size, and burned white hot. Huge streams of incandescent gas and plasma were streaming from its surface, and it seemed to be throbbing gently as they watched it. A signal from the space station came over on sound only, very distorted through the crackle of static.

"Attention evacuation ships! Auriga is going critical." The signal was shut off in a howl of noise.

As Laurel watched Auriga, a whole section of its surface was expelled into space, and the star became dazzlingly bright, almost unbearably so.

"This is it," Van declared simply. "Nova star." He looked at the clock and Laurel followed his gaze. Since Dr Lindberg's last communication, only twelve hours had passed. Van put the schematic on screen. The red dots were further out than they had been and a few of them had already jumped into quantum space. But the others were still there, straining their way outward from the star.

There was something new. Radiating out from the star was a blurred white circle; the blast wave of a nova star, consuming everything in its path.

11. Sacrifice

Laurel stared with horrified fascination as the white circle on the screen made its seemingly leisurely way outwards to where the red dots indicated the remnants of the armada struggling to outrun it. She watched as the blast wave reached Akron, beautiful Akron, for so long her home and the seat of her earliest memories. She remembered the graphic she had helped put together, the one which depicted the planet's destruction. Now it was happening for real. She choked back her feelings as the circle of death enveloped the brown and white orb. Akron might be small, but it had been the only planet she'd known. Until her move to the station, it had seen the whole of her life. Now it was gone, the beauty of its dawns and sunsets, its green mountain mists, the Trembling Lake, all gone. Laurel felt as if a small part of herself was being extinguished. The planet which had shaped her would live on only in the memories of those who had known and loved it. The question now was how many of them would survive?

Even as she watched, a couple of the red dots on the edges of the schematic disappeared from screen. They were leaping into quantum space. Many of the others would not make it in time, and when they were hit by the blast they would be consumed. Laurel was speechless at the thought of the loss of life. Van explained the process.

119

"The wave of radiation comes first. It is intense enough to kill everything. The blast wave follows a little behind and will incinerate everything in its path in a storm of incandescent gas and plasma. The only way to escape is to go faster than light; to jump into quantum space."

"And what about us?" Laurel asked, staring at expanding circle on the schematic. "Will we make the jump in time?"

"The ship absorbs radiation, so we have more time than most. But we can't survive the blast itself."

Laurel's heart sank. The space station had nowhere near enough time to make the leap. After all they had done to evacuate the planet, there was no escape for them. She used the controls to contact the space station.

"Akron station," a voice called back, distorted by the static pollution of space. Laurel's heart leapt. It wasn't just Akron station; it was Blake. She knew that voice so well, even across millions of miles and through the distortion.

"Blake, it's you!" she cried. His face appeared on distorted screen. Van fiddled with his controls and both sound and picture stabilized a little.

"You are safe?" an anxious Blake inquired. It was Van who answered.

"Yes, we think so. The ship will absorb the radiation wave, and we should reach clear space before the blast comes."

"What about you?" Laurel asked anxiously. Even through the distortion and signal fade, his face was clearly not optimistic.

"I'm afraid we won't make it. We're too big and too slow. We could maybe just outrun the blast wave, but the radiation will get us long before then." His expression was more resigned than gloomy. It had a set appearance to it.

Laurel felt on the verge of tears, although she choked them back. Apart from Van and her parents, every person she cared about was on that station. Blake himself, of course, but also the people she had worked with and played with during the two years she had been there. Her whole life was about to be wiped out. She couldn't stop her voice trembling as she spoke.

"Blake, how ever am I going to manage without you?" she asked desperately. Blake shrugged and gave her a weak smile.

"Oh, just like you always did. I don't think you ever needed me, but it was fun." Blake smiled weakly. "Goodbye Van," he said. "Look after her."

"Goodbye Blake. I will if I can," Van replied.

"And goodbye Laurel." As Blake said it, Laurel saw him press his hand close up until his fingertips filled the screen. She knew at once what he was trying to do. He was trying to touch fingertips in the Korami farewell ritual.

She pressed her own fingertips to the camera, and touched his fingers on the screen with her other hand, as she knew he would with hers.

"Goodbye Blake," she said softly. As the connection was broken she leaned back feeling drained. She looked at Van, and he at her, but there was nothing to say.

While Van busied himself with some calculations, Laurel stared at the screen, without seeing it. She was reliving her life on the station, the life which had freed her from her parents' home on Akron, which had given her the chance to be herself and express herself for the first time. It was her home, and Blake had played a larger part in her life there than anyone else. Now her home, and Blake, and everything and everyone she cared for was headed to extinction. It would all be snuffed out like a candle in infinity, as if it had never been. But Blake was right about one thing. It would all continue to exist in her thoughts.

She was pulled out of the thoughts by Van, who rested a hand on her shoulder.

"I've been doing some thinking, too," he said, indicating his calculations.

121

Laurel looked up. She had learned to interpret those strange amber eyes. This was something serious. She pulled herself back to the present with an effort.

"I propose we don't let things take their natural course," Van said. "If I could position my ship at some distance behind the station it could act as a radiation shield. We could buy the space station more time. According to my calculations, we can buy them enough time to reach clear space and make a quantum jump."

Laurel sat bolt upright, her head reeling.

"Then let's do it!" she exclaimed with joy, before catching the look on Van's face. "What's wrong?" she asked. Van looked almost apologetic.

"We can save the station, but not ourselves. We won't be far enough to beat the blast wave. The ship will be incinerated."

Laurel stared at him and thought hard. They could save themselves and the station would be destroyed, or they could save the station and would themselves be destroyed. It didn't seem like a fair choice.

"Once we head to the station, you can take your shuttle on an intercept course. We can patch up the wing, refuel it. You wouldn't need much manoeuvrability to get to the station, you'd have a fair chance of getting there on a set trajectory."

"How good a chance?" asked Laurel. She didn't like the sound of this. Van looked down.

"A fair chance," he replied. "You might make it."

"I'll take that chance," she said, "but what about you?"

"I'll die with my ship," said Van simply. As Laurel started to protest he calmed her. "It's a good trade from my point of view. I might as well do something worthwhile for the people I value. I know how much the station and its people mean to you. If I don't do it, I'm not sure I rate the life ahead of me all that much anyway. As I told you at the Trembling Lake, I think I'll wake up again with none of my memories. I'll forget everything I've learned, everyone I've learned to value. I won't be giving up so much. I might as well save others instead."

Laurel was shaken by the thought that Van was prepared to sacrifice his own life to save the others. She understood that the offer he was making was not hers to turn down. She nodded, understanding once more how lonely life must be for him.

Van played with the controls, and Laurel felt the slight tug of its acceleration as it changed course. She watched the schematic on screen as the ship moved in an arc to put it between the station and the ever-approaching white circle radiating from Auriga. She made a decision.

"I'm not going in the shuttle." It was firm and final, and Van's face registered that he could tell that.

"If you stay here we both die," he said mildly.

"I can die here, with the comfort of a friend. Or I can try my chances in a space shuttle I've already crashed once today. I'd rather die with you than alone in space." She looked up, and spoke in almost a whisper, "I think I'd rather die with you than with anyone else."

Van gazed back at her, unable to argue but desperate not to accept. He was interrupted by a communication from the space station. It was Dr Lindberg. His face was drained, his fate sealed.

"You're moving back into danger. What's happening?"

Van outlined the plan, which was received in stony silence. Dr Lindberg's face kept fading, and streaks of interference occasionally clouded across it. But there was no mistaking his expression when he finally spoke.

"The plan would work, I admit. And it's a generous offer. But the price is too high. I cannot allow it."

Van was amused. "I always did have a problem with authority," he told Dr Lindberg. "Since I've already taken the necessary action, what you will allow is of only marginal relevance."

Lindberg nodded. "This is difficult for all of us," he told them. "We've spent the last few hours in the belief that they would be our last. Now you've given us another chance of life, but at a cost I find it difficult to deal with." He stared down at his hands, unable to make eye-contact whilst he came to a decision. "Very well, I owe a responsibility to everyone on the station. I'll take a leaf out of Tremayne's book and divert life support power to the engines. We can manage a few hours of discomfort. The least we can do is to maximize our chances."

"Then it is agreed," Van announced, and the communication was severed.

After all the anxiety about escaping the first wave of the explosion, Laurel now found herself waiting impatiently for it to hit. When it finally did the effect was anticlimactic; all she could feel was a slight tremor in the ship. Van checked his instruments and confirmed that the ship was absorbing the particle storm. No lethal rays would reach either the two of them or, more importantly, the station and its crew.

It was then another waiting game. The red dot that was the station inched its way towards clear space, while behind it the blast edged inexorably closer.

"Soon," Van said. Laurel nodded.

Suddenly Lindberg came on screen, his face triumphant.

"We're clear!" he announced. "Standing by to jump. Goodbye, and a final heartfelt thank you." And then he and the station were gone. Van pointed to the schematic, but Laurel could see for herself that the big red dot had disappeared. She could also see that the white circle was almost upon them. She stood up.

"I'm afraid," she told Van.

11. SACRIFICE

"Me, too. It won't take long." They looked at each other. Finally Laurel broke the silence as the ship began to rock against the oncoming circle of death.

"Van, will you hold me?"

Yes he would, and did so as the blackness engulfed them.

* * * * *

"Are we dead?" asked Laurel.

"I don't think so," replied Van.

She couldn't see anything in the total blackness. The familiar hum and throb of the ship was gone, just an eerie silence in its place. She could feel Van's heartbeat against her, and she could feel her own heart beating.

"What happened?" she asked.

"I don't know. The blast from the star hit us."

"Are we moving?"

"I don't think so, I can't see or hear anything."

They remained silent a while longer. It seemed they had been lifted together out of space and time. Nothing else existed except themselves. Laurel was infinitely glad that she had chosen to be with Van. To face this alone would be unbearable.

"I think we might be in quantum space," Van finally remarked, "though it's hard to see how we can be."

"But we were too close to the star and its distortion field."

"That's right," said Van. "But I can't think of any other explanation."

"How long will this go on?" she asked.

"I don't know. Maybe forever," Van suggested. Laurel shuddered.

"Perhaps," he continued, "until we stop breathing. Let's stay in each other's arms until we do."

They remained that way for a long, long time.

12. The ship

The screen exploded with stars as they re-entered the universe. Ten thousand dazzling points of light blazed out at them. The contrast with total blackness was as sudden as it was dramatic. Laurel flinched and shielded her eyes as she searched the screen.

"Where are we?" she asked Van, but he was already bending over instruments trying to find out.

"We're still in the globular cluster," he remarked in surprise. Suddenly he looked up at Laurel with an astonished look on his face. "We're close to the station."

As he spoke the image of the station came up on screen, silver against the black of space. Laurel's heart leapt. They had made it. Her home was still there, its people safe. As if to confirm it a voice came over the communicator.

"I don't believe this. Are you safe?" It was Dr Lindberg.

"Cadet Mackay and citizen Van present and correct, sir, reporting for duty," Laurel replied before Van had a chance to speak. Lindberg's face came on screen, in clear and prefect reception without a trace of interference.

"How in the stars did your ship manage the jump?" demanded an incredulous Dr Lindberg. He was joined by an excited Blake, squeezing him to one side in his eagerness to get to the screen.

"Laurel!" cried Blake. "And Van. You both made it." A huge smile lit up his face.

"We don't know how, but somehow the ship jumped," replied a puzzled Van.

"There really is no end to the ship's mysteries," Lindberg cut in. "But the main thing is you're both safe. Welcome home, Cadet Mackay."

"Did the other ships make it?" she asked.

A cloud briefly crossed Lindberg's face.

"Not all of them. A few stragglers were caught in the radiation and the blast." Then his face brightened. "But most of them made it, including the *Arcturus*. It was the last one to jump ahead of the starburst."

Now it was Laurel's turn to light up. Her parents were safe! She turned to Van with joy on her face. He smiled in turn. There was one jarring note when Laurel asked about the *Lodestar*. Blake shook his head.

"No word, I'm afraid. We don't think they survived. If he hadn't stayed to take the Torquada he could have made it."

A wave of guilt engulfed Laurel. If they had not stolen Tremayne's CAG and bargained over its return he might well have made it safely away. She explained how he had stayed behind to take some evacuees.

"In that case," responded Blake, "he'll be remembered as a hero. Quite a sacrifice."

She and Van were the ones treated like heroes. After they docked with the space station, they came out to find most of the station's population crowded in the bay. The applause was loud and heartfelt. Van was confused and embarrassed, and offered a nervous half-smile in return. As they walked past the crowd, people reached out to touch his arm or pat him on the shoulders or on his back. Laurel was deeply touched by the sincerity of their tribute. He had offered to sacrifice his life to save them, and it was not a gesture easily forgotten.

Tremayne might indeed go down in history as a hero, but he clearly had no intention of doing so just yet. About an hour later, the hail came through loud and clear. Van and Laurel were with Blake and Dr Lindberg in the communications room.

"*Lodestar* calling Akron station." And there on screen was Tremayne himself. A cheer went up in the station's communications room, which Tremayne acknowledged with a gracious nod and a theatrical wave of one hand. He looked sweaty and dirty, but triumphant, and held a small girl on his hip.

"Now that's what I describe as a good call," he declared contentedly. "When it came time to show cards we had just enough." He looked more serious for a moment, then added, "Though I concede it was close."

"Perhaps the Torquada brought you luck." Laurel suggested.

"Alas, she stayed on Akron. There wasn't room in the end. In any case, after a million years everyone is due some retirement." He stroked the hair of the little girl in his arms and was rewarded by a huge grin.

Laurel was surprised. So the relic had died with the planet. It seemed fitting.

"Who's the girl?" she asked.

Tremayne looked thoughtful. "Harmony," he replied, trying the name out for the first time, "Harmony Tremayne." The little girl grinned again as he looked at her.

Laurel raised her eyebrows. "Do you think you can keep her?"

"Oh yes. I'll get the best lawyers that money can buy," said Tremayne confidently. "And that's all of them."

Van spent most of his time in his ship. He claimed he wanted to find out how it had saved them against the odds, but Laurel suspected that the real reason was to avoid the adulation which greeted him everywhere on board the station. She found it amusing that people would stop to thank him and ask to have themselves pictured with him, but Van clearly found it hard to deal with.

She sought out Van aboard his ship, and found him still running diagnostics. He looked up and nodded as she entered.

"I don't understand a quarter of what this ship's capable of. It's almost as though it's been designed to stop me finding out," he commented ruefully.

Laurel sympathized. The entire technical staff of the station had failed to make any progress either. The black ship had resisted every attempt to find out its secrets.

"Somewhere in this ship might be the key to who I am and where I came from." He banged a fist lightly against the console. "But I don't know how to even start finding it. The databases are all encoded, the systems like nothing else I've seen. If only the thing could speak."

As he said the words there was a slight vibration within the ship, and the lights dimmed briefly before brightening again.

A calm, measured voice spoke out into the room. Laurel couldn't tell where it came from because it seemed all around them.

"Perhaps it is time for some of your questions to be answered," the voice said evenly. Laurel caught her breath, and she saw Van freeze at the sound of it.

He was the first to recover his composure.

12. THE SHIP

"Is that the ship's computer?" he questioned. His eyes darted around, unsure where to look when addressing a disembodied voice.

"Indeed, though it would be more accurate to say that I *am* the ship. Every molecule of it is part of me. There are lesser computers which control the ship's systems and which store its records, but my intelligence is derived from the ship's entirety."

Laurel exhaled slowly. The impersonal, level tones were somehow thrilling. Her skin tingled at the strangeness of it.

"You are wondering how you were able to escape the exploding star," the voice continued in the same measured tone. "You already understand that the ship was able to absorb the radiation wave. Similarly, it can neutralize a star's distortion field. It can jump into quantum space much closer to a star than a normal ship."

Van nodded thoughtfully. It made sense.

"But you took the decision yourself without any orders?" he challenged.

"Yes," replied the voice. "I direct this ship. I can choose to accept your instructions, but I can also override them."

Van seemed taken aback by the information. Indeed, Laurel herself was somewhat shaken by the thought that the ship, not the pilot, had the ultimate authority.

"Who built you?" It was Van who asked the question, but the same thought had occurred to Laurel.

"Your people did, Van," the ship answered. "I was the highest product of their technology at the time, but it was long ago."

Laurel watched Van as he struggled to make sense of the information. Then a wistful expression came over his face as he put the one question that mattered most to him.

"Why am I here?" he asked. There was a distinct pause.

"You are being punished," replied the ship.

131

"What?" Laurel was incredulous. Van looked pretty surprised, too. "What did he do?" she demanded.

"It is not what he did," the voice continued, "but what he is. Van was bred for one purpose only. To foment a revolution." Van looked numb, as if overawed by the revelation, but the ship continued its explanation.

"Van's culture had enjoyed a thousand years of peace. But there were dissidents who wanted to overthrow its tranquil order and launch it upon a career of galactic conquest. They created a few people like Van, individuals of great resource, intelligence and fighting skills. Rebellion was built into their very nature; it was their only purpose. They were engineered to resist authority and to overcome it."

"What happened?" asked Laurel in a still small voice.

"The attempted uprising failed, but only narrowly and after great destruction and loss of life. The others like Van were all killed in the action. He was thought too young for combat, and was the only one of the special group to survive. When it was over Van was seized and exiled to prevent further disorder."

"But that's not fair!" cried Laurel. "He's not guilty of doing anything."

The ship spoke directly. "In his culture, fairness is of less concern than the outcome of events. Van is being punished to prevent an undesirable outcome. Fairness does not come into it. Given his qualities, there was nothing else they could do."

Laurel seethed at the injustice of punishing an innocent boy for the crimes of others, but Van had a more pertinent question.

"What is the form of this punishment?" he asked.

"It is exile from everything and everyone you knew. You have been sent on a series of voyages, long voyages. Every seven years you have faced a trial and an ordeal. Each has taken you through momentous events. After each one your memory has been erased and the records of the ship expunged."

12. THE SHIP

"And I suppose this goes on forever," said Van wearily. He sat down and put his head in his hands. "It would have been better if I had died in saving the station." He looked utterly disconsolate. Laurel moved to put a comforting arm around his shoulders.

"Nothing is forever," said the ship. Laurel and Van both looked up in surprise.

"There have been dangers at every trial," the ship continued, "and the people who sent you on these voyages did so reluctantly because they feared you would not survive. They had no other option. But they did allow for the possibility that time and circumstance might change you. They built into the master program of this ship the ability to recognize if you reformed sufficiently that you no longer constituted a danger either to their own culture, or to other civilized and settled peoples."

"And how is Van expected to know when that happens?" demanded Laurel. She was still fuming at the unjust punishment meted out on an innocent boy.

"Van is not expected to know," replied the ship. "It is enough that I know. The punishment and the testing are now over. There will be no more seven-year sleeps. No more trials. No more punishment."

"But why?" asked a puzzled Van.

"You have changed. You were ready to sacrifice your own life to save others. You have never done that before. The readiness of someone to die with you and for you is another sign of your change. The punishment is now over. You are free to embark upon your own life. From here the future is no longer determined for you. It will be what you decide to make it yourself."

* * * * *

As the black ship drifted slowly away from the station's docking bay, Blake's face came on screen.

133

"This is it, Laurel. Last chance to stay with us," he said.

Laurel laughed. "Good try, Blake. But this is really it, going out into the universe. Everything I ever wanted. I'll keep in touch, of course. I'm sure I'll have countless adventures to bore you with."

"I wish you'd stayed, Laurel," he remarked plaintively.

"So do I, Blake," she said softly. "But I also need to go, and I've made my choice."

Lindberg's face appeared. "We wish you well, Laurel. Remember there's a special place in our hearts for both you and Van. We'll miss you both."

Van had his own message for Dr Lindberg. "Thank you for all the help, Dr Lindberg," he said. "You will find a small package on your desk. It is a farewell present," he announced.

Lindberg disappeared briefly, then reappeared holding the package.

"May I ask what it is?"

Van tilted his head. "A Nobel Prize," he said simply.

Lindberg paused, then looked up in puzzlement.

"It contains a sample of my DNA, together with my full approval for your use of it in any scientific research."

Lindberg's eyes slipped out of focus. Laurel could see he was contemplating the possibilities. She watched his fingers playing absent-mindedly with the package they held. Finally he looked up.

"Van, this is the most handsome thanks you could have given. It isn't a Nobel Prize yet, but I assure you I will do everything in my power to make it one."

And then the goodbyes were over and it was time to leave. Laurel looked over the ship. The refitted quarters were small, but she already regarded it as yet another home. A thought occurred to her as she settled in.

12. THE SHIP

"Van, we ought to name the ship. We shouldn't cross space in a nameless ship. What do you suggest?" she asked. But it was the ship which replied. Once again the disembodied voice whose strangeness Laurel still found thrilling spoke to them.

"I already have a name." it told them. "It is a name honoured in the stories which people have told to each other over the centuries. It is the name of the ship which bears its lone occupant down the great oceans of eternity. It is a name as old as legend."

"And what is that name?" Laurel began.

But before she could finish the question the ship jumped into quantum space, taking its occupants toward a new destination and a new adventure.

THE END

Epilogue

In humanity's voyages of exploration the story has been told many times and in different ways.

In 1641 Captain Vander Decken was returning from the Dutch East Indies in a ship laden with gold, spices and other precious cargo. His ship encountered a ferocious storm off the Cape of Good Hope. Refusing to put into safety, the Captain sailed into the teeth of the storm swearing he would round the Cape even if he had to sail the seas for all eternity.

The gods punished his blasphemous oath by condemning him to sail alone in his ship for all time. In some versions he is allowed ashore briefly every seven years, to be freed from his curse if he finds the love of a woman prepared to die for him and with him. Some say he was saved, but others tell us that the *Vliegende Hollander* still roams the great oceans of eternity, bringing a curse upon everyone who sees it.

ALSO BY MADSEN PIRIE

Children of the Night

Rebellious elements of the nobility and the church threaten the realm, as does the sinister sect known as The Children of the Night. Mark, the orphan cathedral boy, teams up with Gene, the rich girl dragonfly pilot. With them goes Quicksilver, the telepathic rat, and Calvin, the talented young engineer. When they learn of the destruction to be unleashed, they embark on a perilous journey to thwart the impending disaster...

Published by Artic Fox Books, May 2007